Lost & Found

Sara J. Kuhrman

i

ACKNOWLEDGMENTS

First of all, I would like to thank Rhonda Kuhrman, my wonderful mother and partner in business. Without you, Mama, I wouldn't be able to do this.

I thank my father, William Kuhrman, for introducing me to the legacy of books and knowledge that you lived, your memory will remain in my heart always.

I thank my best friend, Kathleen, for agreeing to be my cover model. Your rare beauty is as exceptional as our friendship.

To Sue Ann Dobson, you are my trusted mentor and friend, your careful guidance has shaped who I am today.

Thank you to my little sister who is my biggest fan. I love you, Francie.

Monica, you are a beautiful, endless source of inspiration. This book exists because of you.

Finally, I thank my eternal Lord, the one who granted me the gift of life and the gift of authorship. I praise Your name in all that I do.

-Sara Kuhrman

Chapter One

I gritted my teeth and muscled my way through the crowd with my shopping cart. The store wasn't really too busy for a Saturday afternoon, but there was a throng of old ladies standing around chatting and blocking the way. I caught the strain of the conversation, which involved something about adult diapers and multivitamin supplements. Grimacing, I muttered, "Excuse me."

One of the ladies glanced at me but refused to move, continuing to chatter away to her companions. "My cat had to go to the vet last week," she twittered, sounding like she had cotton balls jammed up her nostrils. "He swallowed a hairball."

The other ladies gasped and put their hands over their hearts. "Oh, dear, that's awful, Beatrice," another one said loudly. They continued to obstruct the way, and I began to lose my patience. I didn't like crowds, and I certainly didn't appreciate my whole afternoon being farted off by a bunch of old biddies that were blocking the only avenue to where I needed to go next. I was generally laid-back but had a bit of a temper when necessary.

"Excuse me!" I tried again, my voice coming out in a frustrated growl, losing my temper. "Unlike you people, I'm trying to shop!"

This got their attention. Beatrice stopped twittering away about her hairball-ailed cat and they all stared at me, lip-lined mouths agape with disapproval. They moved aside and I brushed past with my heavy grocery cart, a grim set to my thin pink lips. I heard one of them mumble something about

1

how disrespectful the younger generations were. I was slightly irritated, but I didn't bother to retort, just simply walked on, very grateful to have the aisle finally clear or obstruction. I was twenty-three at the time, average sized with an athletic, compact build, light brown hair falling to my shoulders and wide blue eyes.

When I finished shopping, I proceeded to the checkout lanes. I scanned in vain for an open lane, but didn't seem to find one.

"Hey, Cindy!" someone called. I turned and squinted to see who was calling my name and saw that it was one of the cashiers; she was at a lane that had a closed sign. "Over here!"

I wheeled over and saw that it was Grace, one of the girls stationed down the hall from me at work. I worked as a secretary for a divorce lawyer, and she worked as the secretary for a bankruptcy lawyer. I waved to Grace and gave a sigh of relief when she said that she would check me out. "I was just about to close," she explained. "But I'll take you. You look like you're in a hurry."

"Thanks," I told her. "You know how much I hate crowds."

Grace and I chatted as she scanned my items through, but I really didn't feel like talking. I was tired and just wanted to go home and get some sleep. I mustered up a smile and managed to be pleasant.

"Have a good night, Cindy," she told me. "You'll make it."

"You too," I replied with a smile. "I'll try."

I was just about to leave the store when I saw something glinting out of the corner of my eye. I turned and saw that it was a silver chain, attached to a woman's purse, which was sitting on the ground. *Someone must have lost their purse*, I thought to myself. Ordinarily I would have just moved on but I figured that whoever lost it must be frantic, so I parked my cart and went over to the purse. It was a clunky leather thing

2

with a silver chain strap and the initials "T.C.G." inscribed on it. Inside was a card with chicken-scratch handwriting and ink blots with an address on it. No name or phone number, just an address. Sighing, I picked it up, and decided that the best I could do as a citizen was to drop by T.C.G.'s house later and try to return her purse, since her house was not too far from my own. I put the cumbersome, somewhat gaudy handbag into my cart and exited the store.

Chapter Two

After I finished my frustrating grocery-shopping extravaganza, I headed home to my empty house. It was kind of lonely sometimes, living alone, with only the company of my aging German shepherd, Butler. I was extremely grateful to have him with me, but I still wished for more sometimes. I had never been popular with the boys, or ever really cared, in fact I had only had one boyfriend and it ended catastrophically, so I just simply never tried again, or found anyone worth my time. I decided to cook some spaghetti for dinner, and although it was bland and boring it was better than nothing. I fed Butler, and we sat in silence for a while.

Looking out the window, I could see that it was getting dark, but I still wanted to return the purse before I put it off any longer, simply because I didn't want to have to do it later. I put the dishes in the sink, patted Butler on the head, and put my coat on. I checked the time and it was seven-thirty. Kind of late but not too late, I thought. I pulled my hair back into a ponytail and threw the strap of my purse over my shoulder, taking the woman's purse with me as well, and pulling my car keys out from hiding. I locked the door of my house behind me and walked down the stairs, climbing into my battered black Nissan Versa. It was a drab car, but I didn't care, since it worked.

I pulled out the tattered address card and turned onto the main street, putting on my turn signal for left. Cars whooshed by and the pleasant night air whistled in through my open windows. I turned on the radio and one of my favorite songs was playing. Quietly singing along and basking in the crooning glow of the singer's voice, I drove around until I found the correct street. I found that the house, 420 Burma Ave, was a slightly weathered white house set back from the road and veiled in trees. As I started up the muddy, bumpy driveway, it got darker, and when I pulled up at the house I could barely see. There was a light on inside the house, and I could see a shape through the translucent lacy curtains. Perplexed by the lack of light and activity, I clutched the purse and cut the motor. When the sweet, serene music stopped, I was stunned by the silence, the only sound of crickets chirping in the grass. Taking a deep breath, I walked up the stairs to the house and knocked on the screen door. There was no reply, so I knocked again, louder and harder. Suddenly, the night air was pierced by a sharp shriek.

"Frank, you bloody bastard!" a female voice hollered. "Get off my property before I shoot your nuts off!" I recoiled in shock as the screen door was thrust open, and I could barely make out the shape of a woman. I opened my mouth to explain that I wasn't Frank, when I felt the cold tip of a gun pressed against my temple.

"Jesus Christ!" I swore, jumping back and stumbling down the stairs with a clatter, knocking something over. A moment later, the porch light flicked on, and I sat trembling on the steps. Unconsciously, my jaw dropped open when the figure stepped into the light, and I brushed my light brown bangs out of my face and looked up. The woman who had almost blown my brains out was probably around my age, and the most beautiful woman I had ever in my life laid my eyes on. She had long, wavy black hair that streamed down her back, long-lashed, misty, sad grey-green eyes like an Irish moor, red lips and a mole on the side of her mouth that made

5

her even more beautiful. She was thin, almost too thin, but had a pleasant curve about her that kept her from looking emaciated.

"Goodness, I'm sorry," she told me, her eyes wide. She offered me a delicate hand, and with surprising strength, gently pulled me to my feet. "I couldn't see without my glasses." Once the dust was brushed off, she asked me what she could do for me.

I handed her the purse. "I believe this is yours?" I asked. "The address on the card was this one."

She took the purse and gasped. "Thank you so much!" she exclaimed. "I've been worried sick. I left this at the store the other day. Please do come in."

She held the door open and I followed her into her modest and barren living room, where she offered me a seat. I looked around at the pale, tattered lace curtains, bare dark hardwood floor, and sagging grey couch, as well as a few armchairs. "Can I get you some coffee?" she asked me. "I have some on the burner in the kitchen."

"Sure," I accepted, and she soon returned with two steaming mugs of amber liquid. She took a seat across from me. I noticed that she was dressed in a very pretty lace adorned black shirt that dipped down, showing a slice of her smooth olive skin, and grey pants with the cuffs rolled up. Her feet were bare, fingernails and toenails painted black.

"Listen, I'm very sorry," she explained, a wrinkle in her brow and her pretty lips pursed with apprehension. "I have been getting pestered by my psychotic ex-husband, and I couldn't see in the dark. I don't get many visitors, you see. I hope you will forgive me."

I smiled at her. "It's all right," I told her. "I'm just glad you didn't blow my brains out with that thing. I'm Cynthia Washek, by the way. Call me Cindy."

She took my hand and shook it gently. "Teela Grant," she answered, those piercing grey-green eyes of hers sizing me up and probably mentally hacking me into pieces and figuring me out. Her analytical gaze unnerved me a bit, but also fascinated me. I looked away but looked back at her again, studying her as she studied me. "...and just to ease your fears, it wasn't even loaded," she added.

"Oh," I breathed a sigh of relief. "That's good to hear." We talked for a little while longer, before I told Teela that I should probably be getting home. She waved goodbye to me and again apologized profusely for frightening me with the gun. She also offered me a generous reward for returning her purse, and I thanked her greatly but gently refused, touched because I knew she wasn't rich by the modest condition of her living room and the rest of her house. I left her house and hopped into my Versa. As soon as I was en route back to my house, I realized how much I wanted to see Teela again. Although she had nearly blown my brains out with a rifle, she seemed like a very interesting person and there was something about her that I couldn't forget. Wow, that woman has a lot of problems, I thought to myself, and imagined how horrible it must be to feel so hunted by a man that it would be necessary to threaten callers with guns, loaded or not. She had explained that she wasn't usually a big fan of weapons, but she was desperate to protect herself, a single woman living alone. I recommended that she get a guard dog, and she beamed when I showed her my favorite picture of Butler and I that I kept in my wallet.

When I got home, I curled up in front of my fireplace with a cup of coffee and cuddled with Butler. He looked up at me as if to ask how it went, and I chuckled and scratched him behind the ears. "Well, But," I told him with a smile. "I nearly got shot, but it went fine."

Chapter Three

I was sitting at my desk on an ordinary Monday morning, filing some papers for my boss, Attorney Jim McGavin. It was irritating busywork, and I had been swamped the past week or so. I sat at my cluttered desk, papers piled up all around me. I took a sip of my coffee and the phone rang, startling me, and causing me to spill coffee all over my lap. Shit, I muttered to myself, dabbing at the stain on my khaki pants and watching the steaming liquid drip onto the worn, dusty, industrial-grey carpet beneath my swivel chair. The walls were plain white with a few depressing pictures on it, but generally the office was pretty bare. Attorney McGavin had a huge, lush office, while I, his poor wretched secretary, had to sit out in the gloomy foyer. I was typing away furiously when the intercom buzzed. I looked at the caller ID, and it was Maria, the receptionist. I pressed the talk button. "Yes?" I inquired.

"Cindy, Mr. McGavin's 9:30 is here. Will you come and take her to the office?"

"Okay," I answered, and rose, hoping that the client wouldn't mind my coffee-stained pants. I reapplied my lip gloss and pulled my hair back again, trying to look presentable. I pushed in my swivel chair and started to the lobby. When I entered the lobby, my heels clicked on the floor. I walked over to Maria's desk and asked her where the nine-thirty client was. She pointed to someone behind me, and I turned to look, nearly losing my breath when I caught her eye. Teela. She looked positively stunning today, dressed in a scoop-neck black ruffled shirt and black pants, the clothes clinging to her small frame and cupping her curves in a way that could only be described as majestic. Her inky hair was swept into a hairclip, with wispy tendrils dangling in her face. She wore her black-framed square glasses and large, thick, almost gaudy silver hoops as well as a stainless steel gothic cross around her neck, something a biker might wear. Her lips were sealed with gloss, but no lipstick. When I looked at her, she smiled ever so slightly and lifted a hand. I started to walk over, feeling kind of hopped up and jittery, and tripped over my own feet, barely avoiding falling flat on my face at her feet. Too much coffee this morning, I thought to myself, shaking my head, disgruntled.

"Fancy seeing you here; I guess I don't need to introduce myself," I said amiably, grinning at Teela. "I'm Mr. McGavin's secretary. Just come this way."
Teela dipped her head with a smile and followed me without a word. She wore a pensive look, as if she was thinking of something, and I chattered away. She wasn't at all unfriendly with me, but simply listened, studied me.
"I take it that you're not a big talker," I commented offhandedly. "Sorry, I can just go on and on."

Teela looked at me with twinkling eyes. "You're right, I'm rather taciturn," she answered graciously, her lips curving ever so slightly. I still felt off-balance, and nearly stumbled again. "But it doesn't bother me, I enjoy listening."

Soon, we reached Atty. McGavin's office, and I wanted to keep talking to her, but reluctantly I knocked on the door. "Mr. McGavin, your nine-thirty is here."

"Just a moment," McGavin answered, his voice muffled through the thick wooden door. I figured he must be finishing up a phone call or something. Before he came to the door, I turned to Teela. "It was nice to see you again," I told

9

her and offered my hand for a handshake. "I'm glad you don't have a gun pressed to my head this time."

Teela laughed merrily and gently shook my hand. Her hand was soft and smooth, and light as a feather. "Good to see you, Cindy," she said in her soft murmur, before Atty. McGavin opened his door.

When the door clicked open, he assessed Teela with obvious admiration in his eyes. "Good morning, Miss Grant," he said amiably, but I could see the hunger gleaming in his eyes. He shook her hand professionally, but I could see it written all over his face how much he would love to strip off all of Teela's clothes and ravage her luscious body. Personally, I thought McGavin was a bit of a prick, a pain to work for, but he seemed to get a lot of clients and work hard.

Teela returned his handshake with caution and cool professionalism. "Good morning, Attorney," she replied, her voice even but ever so cool. I had a feeling that Teela had been appointed McGavin and not chosen him personally, because although he was a good lawyer he was a freakin' pain in the heinie.

"Right this way," he motioned her into the office, but before he closed the door I heard him tell her to call him Jim. I didn't hear what Teela's reply was, because the wooden door clicked closed with a hollow *thwunk*.

I sat down behind my desk and logged back into the computer. Although I returned to work, I thought of Teela and how rough it must be to be in her situation. There was something about her that caught me every time, nearly stopped me in my tracks when I looked at her. I couldn't really describe what it was. Something about her taciturn, soft-spoken nature, her slight build and softly gothic appearance. Maybe it was the way that she looked at me, looked at anyone for that matter, that piercingly analytical moor-grey gaze that studied and knew. I felt like she could read my soul when she looked at me like that, and she always got a soft light in her eyes when she was listening. I was pretty good at reading people too, and I could tell that Teela Grant really listened, and probably never forgot anything. There was wisdom and power in those sad grey-green eyes that fascinated and unnerved me. I had no idea why I seemed to be such a mess whenever I thought of her. I, Cynthia Washek, was usually a very organized, focused person, but had bungled the hell out of myself when I had gone to meet her this morning, tripping twice and babbling on like a runaway freight train. Was it sympathy, pity or sincerity in her eyes when she told me she enjoyed listening to me talk? I lifted my hand to wipe my nose and realized that it smelled ever so slightly of her lavender body lotion. When she had taken my hand, it felt like a million fireflies were lightly dancing over my skin. Focus, Cindy, I told myself. What the hell was going on?

Just then, the phone rang and an irate client of McGavin's started yelling in my ear. All of my previous musings vanished and I winced as his ear-piercing shriek cut the air. I swiveled my chair around, scribbling down his laundry list of complaints for McGavin to deal with.

Chapter Four

Teela had to come to McGavin's office more often than she probably wanted to, but I really enjoyed talking to her. We got to know each other very well, and became pretty close friends. It was strange how I was so close with the woman who had nearly shot me.

One day, I was sitting in at my desk, and Teela had just finished her meeting with McGavin. She came out and he put his hand on her back and offered to escort her to the door. It was nearly lunchtime, and he looked at the clock. "Care to accompany me to lunch?" he asked, that predatory gleam in his eyes. I could clearly see that he wished that Teela was his main course. "I will be going to the Golden Swan."

The Golden Swan was an uppity restaurant where only doctors, lawyers, and other insanely rich men brought their clients or dates. I waited for Teela to stammer, stutter, or glance side-to-side looking for a way out, but she handled the situation perfectly without a flaw.

"Thank you, Mr. McGavin," Teela replied graciously, her voice smooth, professional, and cool, without a stutter. "But actually, I was about to ask Cindy."

McGavin looked a bit frustrated and ran a hand over the top of his head. He was a lawyer, obviously not very easily flustered, but I understood why he was thrown off balance by

Teela Grant. I don't think that there was a single person on the planet who wasn't thrown off by Teela Grant. "Well, maybe another time, then, Miss Grant," he amended. "Have a good afternoon."

"You as well, Attorney," Teela answered, very tactically not responding to his 'maybe another time' comment. After McGavin had walked off down the hall, I turned to Teela, astonished.

"You want to go to lunch with me?" I asked, shocked. I half expected her to say that she was just trying to blow McGavin off, but she was true to her word.

"Of course," she said to me, cocking her head to the side and giving me a funny look. "Where do you wanna go?"

I shrugged. "I don't know," I answered. "What do you like, Mexican, Chinese, Italian?"

Teela considered. "I feel like Italian," she said finally. "How about the Italia Diner?"

I nodded with approval. The Italia Diner was a small, family owned and family run Italian restaurant that was cheap but delicious, and not too far from the firm. "Sounds good," I agreed.

"I'll drive," Teela offered. "That way, I'll just drop you off on my way home."

"That's awfully generous of you," I remarked. "But thank you. Don't you work?" I wondered as we walked out to her car, which turned out to be a small, beat-up black Kia Spectra. She opened the door for me and climbed into the driver's seat.

"I work part time," she told me, answering my question as she started the car. "Tuesday, Wednesday, Friday. On my days off, I am an aspiring writer."

I gasped. "Wow, Teela, that's wonderful. What do you write?"

"Mysteries mostly," Teela answered. "I'm not much for all that mushy-gushy romance stuff, I don't know about you."

13

I laughed and nodded. "Me either," I told her. "The characters in those are always so fruity." I crossed my eyes, put my hand on my heart and took a deep breath. "Oh, George," I fake-swooned. "I shall simply wither away and perish without thy undying rose-scented love!"

To my surprise, Teela, who was usually very calm and composed, busted out laughing so hard that tears ran down her face. "Oh, Cindy," she cackled. "I don't think anyone's made me laugh like that for a long time," she said after she finally calmed down.

I bowed. "At your service ma'am," I joked. "'Round the clock comedy."

Just then, we pulled up at the diner and Teela parked close to the door and cut the motor. The diner was a pleasant little place with Formica-topped tables, polished hardwood floors, and kind of a lofty, unfinished appearance with bare rafters and ceiling fans that cast soft light and pleasantly circulated warm air that hummed from the ceiling vents. The stools and booths were all vinyl red and green, white roses in a vase on each table. A hostess met us and gave us a table, a little booth at the far end of the restaurant, near the window. We ordered our drinks and sat quietly while we waited for our food. Teela looked preoccupied, a worried frown on her face, so I gently asked her what was wrong. At first, she shook her head and told me that it was nothing, but I persisted, wanting to help her out.

Finally, she sighed tiredly and looked at me, her eyes heavy with the burdens of her ordeals. "It's my ex, Cindy," she told me. "He just won't leave me alone."

I nodded gravely. "Hm, that's terrible," I sympathized. "What exactly does he do?"

Teela sighed. "He calls me, texts me, and when I don't answer he shows up at my house."

"Well, just don't answer the door," I suggested. "Make him think that you aren't home."

She shook her head emphatically and took a sip of her drink.

"No, then he just circles around my house and peers in the windows."

I shuddered. "Damn, that's creepy," I exclaimed. "Why don't you call the police?"

She shook her head again. "I can't," she answered. She lowered her voice to a whisper. "If they came, they would probably look into my records and find out that about my outstanding speeding tickets."

I slammed my hand down on the table. "Jesus, Teela, you're worried about speeding tickets when you're being harassed by a psychotic maniac?"

She shrugged. "I can't afford it," she explained. "And besides, they might not even take him to jail."

I frowned worriedly and took a long drag of my soda. "Well, I guess, but you still should call. So what did you do?"

Teela shuddered. "Well, eventually I just hid. I ended up taking my sleeping bag and locking myself into the bathroom. I slept in the bathtub."

I gasped. "Your bathtub?" I echoed. "Why your bathtub?"

Teela brushed a tendril of midnight black hair out of her face. "It's the only room without a window," she explained. "And if I have to go to the bathroom, there won't be any type of motion. I just don't want to take a chance."

"Has he ever done that before?" I asked.

Teela shook her head. "No, in the past, he has tried to come during the daytime and be civil. That night that I threatened you with the gun, I was totally a nervous wreck, afraid that he was prowling around my house, and last night he actually was."

"He could get nailed for trespassing," I told her. "I work for an attorney. Why don't you get McGavin to help you?"

She shook her head. "Thanks, Cindy, but I'll manage," she sighed. "You know, no one has ever tried to help me like this before. If it happens again, I will think about going to the police."

I nodded. "Okay, well, it's no problem," I answered.

After that, Teela and I dropped the subject and just had a pleasant lunch, but there was an undertone of uncertainty and discomfort after we had brought up the unpleasant topic. After a while, I could see on Teela's face that she was beginning to forget about her problems and just have a good time. The food was delicious. Teela and I split an Italian stuffed peppers dish and Antoine, the main chef, offered us a special slice of his decadent vanilla angel cake for dessert. After we were done and got the check, Teela whipped out her checkbook and wrote a check, sticking it in the bill book. On the way out of the restaurant, I whipped out my purse and offered to pay her back for my portion of the meal, but she waved her hand elegantly and told me to keep it. I started to protest, but I figured that she really felt like she wanted to pay, so I let her. I didn't want to shatter the moment when she murmured, "Keep it, Cindy." The way she said my name sent shivers up my arm, and I couldn't tell why. We sat in silence for a moment, didn't really talk much until she dropped me off back at the law firm.

"Thanks for lunch, Teela," I told her. "That was so sweet of you."

She beamed; her long-lashed moor-grey eyes soft. "You're welcome," she replied, and I could have sworn that she gave me a soft wink before I climbed out of the car. It was snowing pretty hard when I stepped out of her warm, lavender-scented car into the icy blast, but I pulled up my hood and waved one last time as Teela pulled away. She beeped her horn one more time before flicking on her turn signal and disappearing around the corner.

Chapter Five

Later that night, I was at home, curled up in front of my fireplace with Butler. He was asleep at my feet and I swirled my coffee around in my New Zealand Rugby mug, which I don't even remember where I got it. I watched the embers and flames dance and flicker behind the fire screen and I thought about my day. After I had returned from lunch, McGavin had given me absolute hell for being fifteen minutes late. "Miss Washek," he had thundered. "The reason that I have a secretary is for you to be *here.* Not to be out dilly-dallying and having a midday happy hour!"

Good Whitakers, what a prick the man was. Honestly, I think he was just jealous that I went out to lunch with Teela instead of him. Generally, he was a prick when I was late, but he didn't usually chew me out like this. Major jealousy, of his poor little secretary. How sad. Just because Teela invited me to lunch and blew him off.

Speaking of Teela, I thought. Damn it, that woman messed with my mind. She was hypnotic, captivating, utterly maddening with her inky hair, sad eyes, and ruby-red lips. Thinking of Miss Teela Grant made me open up avenues of my mind and question things about myself that I had never questioned or thought about before. Why did she make me feel this way? Was something wrong with me? Was I a lesbian? Just plain mad? I had no idea, but it was about to get even more intense. I was listening to the radio, some gentle, soothing song that was starting to put me to sleep. I dimmed the fire down and sat on the couch, watching the embers as my eyelids began to flicker and my head began to droop like a wilting daisy. The burgundy cushions offered a resting place and I pulled a worn afghan over myself just as my head hit the cushions and the dim light and sweet swirl of slumber pulled me in.

As soon as I was asleep, I found myself dizzy, floating in a semi-soporific grey mist. Suddenly, I was in a dark, warm room. At first I thought I was alone, but then as my eyes adjusted to the dark, I heard someone moving around and saw that it was Teela, her beautiful eyes soft and hot, dressed in a black lace slip, her lips coated in cherry-red stain. I looked down and saw that I was wearing a filmy white silk dress. Teela glided toward me, getting closer and closer until I could feel her warm breath against my cheek.
"Cynthia," she whispered, and suddenly I was kissing her. It was so hot and wonderful; my dream-self closed her eyes..."

I awoke awhile later, the sensation of Teela's lips against my own slowly dissipating as I flitted in and out of reality, my face pressed into the soft burgundy cushion of the couch, my arms thrown around the pillow. I rubbed my eyes and checked the time. When I got up to go to the bathroom, Butler sleepily raised his head. "Damn, But, it's two in the morning," I murmured, scratching him behind the ears. "Go back to sleep, you silly thing."

Butler just whined and lay back down, closing his eyes. When I got back from the bathroom, I didn't bother to go to my bedroom, only curled up on the couch once more and pulled the afghan over myself, but I couldn't sleep, haunted by my heart-pounding dream. Damn it, Teela! What was I supposed to do now? All I knew was that that dream was wonderful. It hit me like a speeding freight train that I desperately wanted to hear her murmur, "Cynthia," against my lips. I wanted to breathe in her scent and I wanted to lose myself in her endless galaxy of mystery. I wondered for a split second what it would be like. I considered the way she looked at me, her eyes soft and pretty. Maybe it was all in my imagination, all in my insane hopefulness, maybe it was just part of her soft-spoken nature. All I knew was that there was something going on between us, something unexplainable. As much as I hated to admit it to myself, trying but failing to slough it off on looping insanity, I think I was slowly falling in love with Teela Grant, and it was killing me. You're lucky, But," I whispered. "You're a dog, not a misguided gal like me."

But Butler didn't hear me and didn't reply, he was off in doggie dreamland, probably chasing squirrels and catching dog bones in his restored youth. Ah, dreams, I thought. All one can do is dream, if nothing else.

Chapter Six

The next day, I got to work and McGavin was in a really bad mood. He was crabbing at me all morning, giving me a lot of busywork. I wasn't in the mood at all, sort of in a daze, still bewildered and beguiled by my thoughts of Teela and the odd dream that I had had the night before. I was restless, getting up and down to refill my coffee cup, listening to the grind of the pencil sharpener, reapplying my lip gloss, et cetera. McGavin came out of his office and leaned over my chair, something that he was notorious for doing.

"Have you finished those files yet, Miss Washek?" he asked, breathing his coffee breath all over me.

I winced at the strong acidic odor and shook my head. "Sorry, Mr. McGavin," I answered. "I'm slightly preoccupied this morning, having trouble focusing."

He ran a hand over the top of his head. "I can see that," he hissed. "I gave those to you two days ago. Now get 'em done!" with a pound of his fist on my desk he turned on his heel and strode back into his office.

"Right away," I called after his retreating back, and his reply was to slam his office door in my face.

Another one of the attorneys, Bob Pierce, a friend of mine, walked by. "Hi there, Cindy," he called as he walked by. "You look pretty today."

"Thank you, Bob, It's good to hear a pleasant voice for once," I replied.

"Bad day, huh?" Bob asked.

I just shook my head and pointed to McGavin's closed door. "McGavin," I mouthed.

Bob came over and set his coffee down on my desk. "I know," he said, keeping his voice down to be out of earshot. "I shouldn't be telling you this, Cindy, but I heard McGavin's hung up on some girl."

I rolled my eyes. "Figures as much," I answered. "God, he's such a grouch."

"Well, I'd better get going," Bob answered. "Keep your head up."

I thanked him and waved to him as he strode off energetically down the hall. Unlike McGavin, Bob Pierce was young and energetic, always smiling. He was also happily married, unlike McGavin, who was a sour bachelor. No wonder, I thought. I, as his secretary, could barely stand to work for the dude, and I couldn't imagine dating or being married to him. I finished up the briefs, with very much concentration, and timidly knocked on McGavin's door.

"I've finished the briefs, Mr. McGavin," I called.

"Come set 'em on my desk," came the gruff, muffled reply.

I pushed the door open and set the briefs down on his desk, as well as some other work that he had wanted me to get done. I knew I would have to butter him up, because he had been extremely agitated since the Teela incident, and even though it was unfair and unprofessional of him, he still held the power to cut my job singlehandedly if he so wished. He took a look at the briefs and nodded gruffly. "Nice work," he grunted.

Wow. What a compliment. I seldom got anything but snappish orders from him.

"Can I get you some more coffee, Mr. McGavin?" I asked, trying to be further helpful, but he looked up and scowled at me.

"Don't push it, Washek," he grunted. "Get back to work."

"Yessir," I answered, but I knew that I had had a success by getting those briefs done for him.

I was so thankful when lunch hour rolled around, I was absolutely starving. I acted like I was busy working until McGavin disappeared down the hall, and I pulled out my lunch pail and my homemade Swiss cheese sandwich with pickles and mustard on whole wheat. Yum, I thought as I dug in in a very unladylike manner. I felt like I hadn't eaten for days, since I had missed my breakfast this morning busting my ass to get to work on time. I was just wolfing down the second half of my delicious sandwich when my desk phone rang, it was the front desk. I picked it up with a sigh. "Yes?" I asked.

"Call for you, Cindy," Anna, the substitute receptionist told me. "It's urgent."

"Okay," I answered, "put it through," and there was a click when she transferred.

"Office of Jim McGavin, this is Cynthia," I answered.

I was startled to hear a low, soft, familiar female voice come through the phone. "Cindy?" the voice asked shakily, barely audible, heavy with muffled tears. "It's me, Teela."

I was stunned. "Teela?" I gasped. She sounded horrible. "What's wrong?"

She took a shaky breath. "Frank came to my house again last night," she told me. "He leered at me through the windows and had a crowbar with him, threatening to break in."

"Did you call the police?" I wanted to know.

"Yes, I did," Teela answered. "They showed up pretty quickly but he disappeared, ran off. They are currently looking for him, but before they came, he threatened me," her voice broke and she sniffled. "I have no family in town, and I can't stay at my house."

"I'll take you to my house tonight, and you can stay there as long as you need to" I answered. "He won't be able to find you there. Where are you now?"

"I'm at work," she answered. "I hate to burden you, Cindy; my mess isn't your problem."

"Don't be ridiculous, Teela," I said firmly. "After work, have someone bring you to the firm, and I'll drive you home with me. That way, if anyone is following you, they won't be able to find you, won't recognize the car."

"Okay," Teela agreed. "I'll have my friend Aimee drive me over, I know she will," she answered rather tersely, stress I suppose.

"See you at five o' clock," I answered, but before I hung up, she stopped me.
"and Cindy?' she added, her voice as soft as silk.

"Yes?" I returned.

"I just wanted to say thank you for everything," she said softly, almost shyly. Before I could tell her that it was okay, there was a click and the phone was disconnected.

Chapter Seven

It was a little after five and I had my stuff packed up. I put on my brown winter coat, grabbed my bag, and headed out into the spacious lobby of the law firm. I looked around for Teela, and at first I didn't see her. Finally, a saw a slight figure hunched over in a dark corner of the lobby. I went over to her, and she had her black hood up. When I approached, my heels clicked loudly on the tile and she lifted her face and managed a weak smile. Gad, she looked awful. She looked thin and haggard, her angular face streaked with the remnant of many hours of crying. Her cheeks were sunken, her lips were pale, and she had purplish lines under her eyes. She wore no makeup, and was dressed in a dumpy black sweater with the hood up. She wiped her eyes.

"Oh, Cindy," she sighed, rising jadedly off the hard wooden bench. "I'm glad to see you."

I wrapped my arms around her and she returned my embrace, almost clinging to me delicately. "I'm glad to see you too, Teela," I told her. "I'll see that you're comfortable at my house. Did you bring anything with you?"

She nodded and held up a small black tote bag and her purse. "Yeah, I've got the basics in here," she indicated wearily.

"Okay, well, follow me then," I told her. "We'll go out to my car."

Teela nodded and followed me, clutching her bag as if it were her only lifeline. I knew that she must have been through some major trauma to be reduced from a smooth-talking soft-voiced goddess to the frightened, haggard maid that stood before me. I shuddered, thinking about how horrifying it must have been to be in a house alone at night with a man waving a crowbar and leering in the windows, shouting twisted threats with the moon gleaming creepily on his ugly face. Teela had said that they married in haste, and soon after, she realized what a mistake it was. At the time, he seemed to agree, but when Teela filed for divorce he took up alcoholism and simply went crazy, stalking her, calling, threatening, following her around, and of course his finale of nighttime mischief outside of her home. She was beaten down, ragged and terrified for her life. We were silent when we braved the cold on the way to my car, and Teela pulled her hood up to conceal her face, just to be on the safe side, in case we were being followed. Even if we weren't, it was better to be ridiculously cautious than naïve and wrong. As the cold wind slapped us in the face with a hailstorm of icy snowflakes, Teela looked pale and delicate as if she could be swept up and blown away by the polar wind. I fought the urge to hold her steady.

I pulled out my keys and unlocked the Versa from afar. I opened the door for Teela and she climbed into the passenger seat. I dumped her bags into the backseat along with my own, and hopped into the driver's seat. It was nearly dark, so I turned the key in the ignition and the headlights came on, as well as the radio, and my favorite CD was in from before. I turned the heat on full blast, and Teela put her leather-gloved hands in front of the register, warming her thin and icy fingers. It wasn't long before we pulled up at my house. I shut the motor off and Teela and I got out of the car, she was still hooded and bundled up. I fished the key out of my pocket and twisted it in the lock, pushing the door open and holding it for my guest. Once we were safely inside my dark, warm house, I shut and locked the door behind us, sealing out the nightmare of the icy blast. Butler, who was sleeping near the door, lifted his head in greeting and slowly came up to Teela to sniff her feet and check her out. He must have liked her, because she patted his head and he licked her shoes and wagged his tail. She smiled when she saw him. "I'm so glad I got to meet you, Butler," she told him seriously, petting him even more.

"He likes you," I told her. "You're welcome here. He's the boss," I laughed.

Teela grinned for the first time in days. "Is that right?" she asked him. He just wagged his tail again and drooled happily on her boots. It was clear that she really loved dogs.

"Here, come get warm," I told her, cranking up the fire in the living room. "And you can leave your shoes here. I'll take your coat."

I hung up her coat in the closet and I put her bags down in the spare bedroom.
"Just let me know when you want to see your room," I told her. "It's kind of modest, just my guest room. Second door on the right down the hall. Bathroom is first door on your left."

"Thanks, Cindy," Teela said gratefully. "Do you mind if I take a shower before dinner? I'd like to wash the day off."

"Sure thing," I answered. "How does homemade tomato soup and grilled cheese sound tonight? There will be salad of course, dressed in lemon and olive oil."

Teela nodded. "Sounds wonderful," she replied. "I can help cook if you like."

"Nonsense," I replied. "Just go take care of yourself, and you can join me when you're done cleaning up."

I headed into the kitchen and clapped on the radio, Teela turned to go freshen up in the bathroom. I got out a frying skillet and a pot for the tomato soup, and began chopping up vegetables. I was humming along to the radio, and soon my simple dinner was done. I stirred and fried, and chopped up lettuce for the salad. I was singing one of my favorite songs full-tilt with my eyes closed when I smelled a slight whiff of lavender and felt the currents shift in the room. I opened my eyes and Teela was standing there, dressed in a black lace-edged scoop-neck, watching me with a slight smile on her lips and a bit of a twinkle in her weary eyes. Although she had been put through the wringer, she still looked gorgeous, slightly more freshened then earlier but still pale and delicate.

"You've a fine voice, Cindy," she told me with her soft-spoken, almost shy sincerity.

I lowered my eyes and stirred the soup some more. "Thanks," I replied with a laugh. "I just sing for fun."

She smiled. "That's the best reason," she answered. "I'll set the table, if you'd like."

I shrugged and brushed a wisp of hair out of my face. "I guess if you want to, go ahead," I told her. She set the places in an orderly fashion, folding the napkins and setting the silverware slowly, methodically, precisely. I watched as she glided around the table with easy grace seemingly in time with the music, silently setting the table as I stirred and chopped and sang. When the grilled cheese sandwiches had browned, the soup was finished, and the coffee had brewed, we sat down at the table. A perfect hostess, I dished up hers first followed by my own. I ate with vigor, but Teela took slow tastes, really learning the flavor of my cooking. "This is delicious," she told me. "You are a talented cook."

I beamed. "Thank you," I replied. "I love to cook. Do you?"

Teela nodded. "Oh, yes, I do," she answered. "I enjoy it very much, but haven't had much time to do it lately."

I nodded sympathetically. "I understand," I told her. "It's been a crazy time for you."

She shook her head. "Undoubtedly," she agreed. "I'm just so glad that I'm free now," she shuddered. "I'll be able to sleep in peace tonight."

"You deserve that much and more," I told her, and poured myself more coffee.
After we had finished eating, we minimally cleared the table and piled the few dishes in the sink. "I'll do those later," I told her. "If you want to go sit down in the living room and get warm, we can."

"I am a slight cold," Teela answered. "I'd love to."

"Would you like a drink?" I asked her. "I have a little red wine."

Teela sighed. "I don't usually drink alcohol," she answered. "But I suppose you can give me a little bit. It might do me good."

I agreed. "Yeah, it's what we need tonight. Go have a seat in there, I'll bring it out."

She turned and walked into the living room, and I was close behind with the two glasses of red wine. I handed the smaller glass to her and then, taking my own, sat down across from her. She sipped it slowly, the flames from the fire dancing and flickering over her pretty face, her moor-grey eyes just studying me intently behind her long black lashes and black framed glasses. Her gaze made me uneasy but thrilled me, making me antsy in my chair, shifting restlessly to find comfort. She must have sensed my restlessness, because she pointed it out to me. "Something wrong?" she inquired softly with a raised eyebrow and concerned look.

I shook my head. "Nah, you just look like you're thinking about something," I stammered.

She shrugged. "I just wanted to thank you," she said softly. "I know I thanked you before, but I will do it again."

"You're welcome," I answered. "It's okay, it really is."
We sat in silence for a few moments; Teela closed her eyes and warmed her thin fingers over the fire. So many different feelings were zinging through the air, having her so close

unnerved me greatly. Maybe it was the wine, but I suddenly felt the urge to break the silence.

"I can't stop thinking about you, Teela," I blurted suddenly.

She turned to face me, her grey eyes soft. She smiled. "Really?" she wanted to know, sounding surprised, but I could feel the hot honeyed tone in her voice, hiding beneath the surface. She sounded puzzled, but pleased. "I wonder why."

"You fascinate me," I told her. "Ever since that night that you nearly blew my brains out with a gun."

She seemed to blush, but she tilted her head, and curved her lips ever so slightly, her analytical moor-grey eyes seeming to trace lazy patterns of heat over my skin.

"You think so, Cynthia?" she murmured. My face flamed red when she said my name and a jolt of electricity swept through me, a live current crackling palpably through the air between us. Her lips shimmered tantalizingly, stained with wine, and I suddenly, seriously wondered if she tasted as wonderful as she had in my dream the other night.

To distract myself, I concentrated on asking her a mundane question. "What's your middle name?" I asked her, but my voice came out with a breathy, restless rasp.

She lowered her eyes. "Constantia," she answered. "What's yours?"

I grimaced. "I have two or three. Grey-Ann and Lynnette," I answered. "Cumbersome, right? Yours is so melodic, so beautiful."

She smiled. "No, I think it is quite fascinating. You know, Cynthia," she said finally. "I have a confession to make."

My breath quickened at the sound of her low, raspy voice. "Yes?" I asked.

She shook her head. "Come here and sit with me," she answered. "I'll tell you in a moment."

Rising on unsteady legs, I went and sat next to her on the couch. The dim firelight played on her face and her black hair fell around her face in a beautiful inky waterfall.

"What is it, Teela?" I wanted to know.

She took a deep breath. "I have been thinking about you too," she murmured, running her hands over my bare shoulders, and sending sparks crackling up my spine.

Boldly, I leaned in and laced my fingers through her wavy black hair, stroking the silky strands. "…and?" I breathed, and she seemed to melt under my touch.

"What would you say," she murmured, her wine and lavender scent winding around me as she kneaded my shoulders. "If I told you that I want you?"

"Teela, I'd say that I simply have to have you," I whispered back and boldly crushed my mouth to hers, tasting her beauty. She turned to molten steel and a soft "ah" escaped her lips. She returned my bold kiss with a venomous, arresting passion and threaded her fingers through my hair. "Cynthia," she whispered against my lips.

Damn, she tasted even better than in my dreams. Her lips tasted like sweet wine and bitter lavender, her scent and her skill intoxicating as her thin and adept fingers kneaded my shoulders. In sheer heaven, I gasped, "Damn, Teela, I love it when you call me Cynthia."

She kept her eyes closed but I could feel her smiling seductively. Gently, she brought me to heaven with her hands.

"Cynthia," she murmured again as she worked her hands up the back of my shirt. "Oh, Cynthia," Butler lay asleep at the hearth, and we were lost from all sense of time, just a cyclone of disoriented, breathless passion. She was beautiful, stunning, unimaginable, and I couldn't get enough. Breathless and exhausted in the weary hours of the morning, we eventually drifted off to sleep in a swirling grey daze.

Chapter Eight

I awoke hunched over, with my face pressed into something soft. I lifted my head to a grey misty light filtering through the curtains. At first, I was completely disoriented, not knowing who I was, where I was or what time it was. I looked down and saw that I was still semi-dressed in my work clothes from the day before, and that what I had been laying on was the arm of the burgundy couch, which in my sleep I had drooled on. I shook my head and wiped my mouth, disgusted. As my foggy memory cleared, I remembered the night before, the drink of wine, the warm fire… and beautiful Teela Grant, in my arms all night long. Suddenly, I sat bolt up and was struck with fear, horrified that Teela was either gone or had left. Had she gotten up and disgustedly decided that she wanted nothing to do with me? Had she come to her senses and decided that she didn't want to go down that road with me? Or worse, had she been taken in the middle of the night? I checked the front door, and there was no sign of jimmying. The windows were secure and nothing was out of place. Maybe she had left silently, wordlessly. I headed through the house frantically, and was dismayed that she was nowhere to be seen.

"Teela?" I called hesitantly, but as I dreaded, only silence awaited me. Sighing and shaking my head, I swigged some mouthwash and decided to freshen up in the shower. Oh, well, I thought. I still had to go to work. I was hesitant to call the police because it didn't appear as if Teela had been kidnapped.

She left me, I thought bitterly. Just to show that she could. Last night she had held me like no one had ever held me before. She knew that I was attracted to her and just twisted my feelings and threw them back in my face. Hell, I didn't even know her that well and I practically threw myself at her feet. "Damn, what a waste," I grumbled as I hopped into the shower and a blast of cold water hit me square in the face. After I had finished my quick and bitter rinse-off, I put my clothes on and combed my hair. Through the bathroom door I thought I heard something moving around, and figured that Butler was getting up, as he often did in the morning. I figured I'd have to let him out soon. A delicious aroma began to wind its way down the hallway, like fresh-cooked breakfast.

Puzzled, I ventured out into the hallway and peered into the kitchen. Sure enough, Teela was standing there at the sink while what looked like pancakes simmered away in the skillet on the stove. There was a pot of coffee brewing on the burner, and there were plates set out at the kitchen table. My first thought was still of my initial worry, and before I could stop myself and be reasonable, I blurted sharply, "I thought you left."

It came out more accusatory and harsher than I intended, and I immediately wished I could take it back, but I was still somewhat miffed at the thought that she had walked out. But when Teela turned around to face me, I was floored and immediately lost my breath at the mere sight of her. She looked much refreshed from the day before, with a clean white lacy V-neck shirt that framed her pretty curves and a sleek pair of black pants. Her cheeks were red, indicating that she had been outside, and light, melting flurries of snow lingered in her silken, inky hair. Her eyes were soft and bright as usual, the face of an angel.

Instead of returning my sharpness, she beamed at me merrily, flipping one of the golden pancakes. "I'm so sorry to have worried you," she explained, an embarrassed flush spreading across her cheeks. "I went out and cleaned off the cars, then decided to make us some breakfast."

Suddenly, I felt like a horrible person. There I had accused her of leaving when she was out cleaning off my car then cooking breakfast. My heart pounded and a lump rose in my throat. I swallowed but could barely speak, feeling like I wanted to cry out of a mix of remorse and gratitude. "Oh, Teela, I'm sorry," I breathed. "I had no idea."

"It's okay, you didn't know," she answered quietly. I was captivated by her beauty, and just wanted to hold her in my arms again, but I had no idea whether she would want that or not. Perhaps she had merely drunk too much wine the previous night and lost her mind. But when she looked at me again, I could see that there was no mistake. Her grey-green eyes flashed over me and filled with that liquid glow.

"I'm sorry, again…" I whispered, still feeling regret for being so harsh to her. But Teela wasn't gonna have any of it. Her lips curved into a smile and she lowered her eyes.

"Don't be sorry. Cut the crap and come here, Cynthia," she murmured; her voice low and silken.

"Teela," I breathed her name almost silently, and could do nothing but stand there, frozen, paralyzed by the queen in front of me. Slowly, I drifted towards her until I was swept into a warm rush of lavender. She laced her fingers through my hair with a delicate tenderness. Her cheeks and nose were cold but her lips were hot and light and sweet against my own. I pulled her closer until my back was up against the sink. Soon, she pulled away and beamed at me.

"Let's eat, Cindy," she told me. "We can't be late for work."

33

She dished up the pancakes and served me first, then gracefully seated herself. I couldn't help but feel a tad miffed that she was worried about work, although she had a practical point. She must have caught my frown, because she winked at me. "Don't worry," she murmured. "We have all night tonight. I won't disappoint."

I simply smiled in return, and took a forkful of pancake. "You seem pretty cool about this whole thing," I told her, referring to our feelings for each other. "It's all pretty new to me."

Teela nodded and took a delicate bite. "Me, too," she admitted. "But after Frank and I were married, I realized something was missing."

I nodded, understanding. "Me, too," I told her. "I was never married, but it never seemed right to me with men. I always found men somewhat barbaric, never attractive."

Teela nodded. "I know what you mean," she said softly. "Frank… he was so… rough, with me," she winced, shaking her head. "I never should have let him touch me."

I looked on her with sympathy, and it nearly killed me to see her so small and vulnerable. "It's okay, Teela," I whispered. "We can't go back, but we can go forward."

Teela looked up and mustered a smile. "That's right, Cindy," she said quietly.

"Let's just see how it goes," I told her. "We don't have to commit to anything, and if you decide that you don't want to stay, you don't have to, but I hope you will."

Teela looked up at me, her eyes wide. "I wouldn't dream of leaving," she breathed.

"Good," I replied. "Because the moment I saw you I knew I couldn't just move on."

She did not reply, but I saw a faint red flush colour her cheeks, and it was clear that she was pleased. After we had finished eating, I offered to clear the table and do the dishes, since she had gone to all the trouble to cook breakfast and clean off the car, but she refused, since it was her day off. I put our dishes in the sink and she said she'd wash them. She walked out to the car with me, despite the fact that it was below zero, wanting to wish me a good day. I climbed into the driver's seat and was about to start the motor when she motioned for me to roll down the window. I complied, and she leaned forward. "Have a good day, Cindy," she said quietly, her grey-green eyes brimming with emotion, and I could see the world itself flickering in her beautiful eyes.

"You too, Teela," I replied, brushing a lock of her inky hair out of her pretty face. She coloured slightly and stepped back with a flicker of a smile, heading back onto the porch. She waved from the front steps as I pulled out of the driveway and I honked once more in farewell.

Chapter Nine

When I got to work, I was preoccupied thinking of
Teela. Her moor-grey eyes had a way of cutting me to the
core and her kiss left me breathless. Whenever she murmured,
"Cynthia" and swept me into her arms it felt like I was the
most important person on earth. No one in my life had ever
made me feel that way. I longed to further my relationship
with her and get to know her in everything. I closed my eyes
briefly and wondered what she looked like in only a scrap of
black lace.

My pleasant daydream was interrupted by the pager on
my desk phone. McGavin. I picked it up. "Yes, Attorney?" I
asked.

"Miss Washek," he intoned. "I would like a cup of
black coffee. Please make one for me."

I rolled my eyes, but at least it was a mindless enough
request. "Okay," I replied, and hung up. I headed down the
hall to where the coffee pot was, and prepared to make a pot
of strong black coffee for my boss. While I was standing
there, Rick Vance, one of the other lawyers, sauntered into
the room, wearing a smug grin. I never liked Rick very much,
he was a spoiled rich boy with black hair and a smug, oily
smile. He was known for his underhanded business dealings
and jerk attitude. He seemed to be popular with the women,
God knows why, and knew it too. Unfortunately, he had taken

an interest in me lately, maybe because I was the one who didn't fall to his Italian shined-shoes feet.

"Why, if it isn't Cindy," he said, rubbing his hands together and looking me up and down sleazily.

"Good morning, Attorney," I replied icily, letting him know that I wasn't interested but wasn't about to lose my professionalism.

But Rick didn't get the hint, for he simply shivered as if he were cold. "Brr," he hooted. "That was *freezing*." He moved closer, and I could smell his nauseating cologne. "Are you *always* this cold, Cindy?" he asked slimily.

I didn't bother to take his bait. Luckily, McGavin's stupid coffee was nearly done. I had no desire to stay and chat with Rick, so I cut out early, poured McGavin a mug of coffee and turned to head back to the office.

"Have a good day," Rick trilled, overly, sarcastically enthusiastic.

"Thanks, you too," I replied, my voice completely even, and I swept off down the hall. When I got back to McGavin's office, the door was about a half inch ajar, but I could hear him through the door talking on the phone in a low voice. It sounded more like a personal call than a business call.

"I can't tell you," I heard him say, then lower his voice. "No, don't," he said menacingly. Generally, I didn't snoop in his business but this growled conversation caught my attention. What could be going on? Was McGavin involved in a drug deal or something?

I pretended to keep working, but secretly I was listening. "Okay, well I'll see how it goes," he said. "And if not, I'll collect the money soon."

There was a pause. "Ten thousand," he insisted. "Not five. Nothing less. Goodbye."

He hung up, and soon the pager on my desk phone buzzed again.

"Surely my coffee is done by now, Miss Washek," he said impatiently.

"Yes, it is, Mr. McGavin," I answered. "I'll bring it right in."

I carefully carried the mug into his office, and set it down on his desk. "Here you go, Mr. McGavin," I told him. "Sorry, I didn't bring it in; you were on the phone."

"Thank you, Miss Washek," he said absentmindedly, and I nearly dropped dead on the floor. Did the guy get a brain transplant or something? I smiled uncertainly.

"You're welcome," I told him, and started out the door, but he stopped me.

"Miss Washek?" he asked, but he didn't sound the least bit irritated.

I turned. "Yes?"

He handed me twenty dollar bill. "I've been under a lot of stress lately," he apologized. "And I haven't been very nice to you. Feel free to take this and go out to lunch today."

I was very surprised and took it with uncertain hands. I tilted my head to the side and stared at him, before I stammered out a thank you.

He smiled jovially. "I'm trying to be a better boss," he explained.

Well, at least McGavin wasn't gonna give me a hard time today, I thought. Maybe the guy had half a heart after all. I looked at the crisp twenty in my hand and sighed. Sandwich shop, here I come, I thought. There was an hour left until lunch, and I was starving. In the morning rush and delirium with Teela, I had forgotten to bring my packed lunch. I was eternally grateful for McGavin's spontaneous streak of kindness and compassion. Was he hitting on me, I wondered. Maybe so. But then again, I had worked for him for nearly a year now and he had never shown interest before. Unless he just had an epiphany moment and decided that Cynthia Washek was the one that he wanted. I grimaced. Gad, I hope not, I thought. One lovesick lawyer sniffing around me was enough, and besides, the male species didn't even interest me. Men were rather repulsive to me, big and barbaric, always wanting to dominate and control women. I remembered the way Teela had held me last night; we had a true emotional bond as best friends. Men, I thought disgustedly. They only feigned an emotional bond so that they could get inside a girl's pants. I was not afraid of men, just not attracted to them. The female aura just fascinated me; women were so soft, so understanding, and so mysterious. Especially Teela, who was waiting for me at home, probably writing on her latest mystery novel, pen held between her glossy red lips. Maybe she was thinking about me. If she was, I wondered what she was thinking. Did she get that smoky-eyed look when she thought of me? I bet she did. I smiled to myself and started shutting down my computer so that I could go get lunch from the restaurant across the street. As I paid for my sub sandwich, a puzzled frown crossed my face. McGavin's phone conversation had really unnerved me, sounding suspicious. Then add the free lunch. Maybe he was trying to buy me off to keep me from finding out his nefarious behavior. *Aw, Cindy,* I told myself. *Cut it out.* I was making too much of this. He was probably talking to a disgruntled client who didn't want to pay. Once I took a bite of heaven on wheels, I completely forgot about it.

Later, after lunch, I dropped into his office to thank him. "Thanks for the lunch money, Attorney," I mentioned. I wondered if I could possibly extract some information about the phone call.

"I'm sorry to pry, Mr. McGavin, but you sounded sort of upset on the phone earlier. Is everything okay?"

McGavin glanced up, somewhat startled, then he shrugged. "Yeah, just the usual stuff," he waved his hand. I didn't press him any further on the issue, didn't feel the need. I headed back to my desk to continue work.

Chapter Ten

When I got home after work, it was around five thirty. I was slightly late because of the snow. I parked the car and unlocked the door. At first, the house was dark and I wondered if Teela had gone out or was taking a nap or something. Eventually, I heard soft music coming from the other room, and I headed into the hallway. I looked through the crack in the door where the sound was coming from, the only sound in the silent house, and I found her sitting in the guest bedroom, her back to me, facing out the window into the slowly approaching night. Her hair was down and she sat nearly motionless, while a really sad ballad played softly on the bedside stereo. I didn't dare to disturb her and tiptoed into the kitchen to start getting dinner ready. I was tempted to ask her what was wrong, but she looked so forlorn, so lost, I thought I'd give her a little time, and then tell her when dinner was ready. I decided to make burritos, rice and salad, because it was fairly simple and would be ready in a few minutes. I poured the rice into a bowl and set it to cook for about twenty minutes in the microwave. I wondered what Teela was thinking of and if something had been bothering her all day. I wanted to go to her, but I was afraid that she would turn me away. Finally, squaring my shoulders and taking a deep breath, I figured that I would at least check up

40

on her. I walked down the hallway quietly, and softly
knocked on the door. "Teela?" I called softly.

I half expected her to tell me to leave her alone, but
she turned around. I was shocked to find her face streaked
with tears, her moor-grey eyes wide and misty. She brushed a
lock of her wavy black hair out of her face and folded her
hands in her lap, but didn't reply, didn't say anything. "Please
tell me what's going on," I pleaded. "I hate seeing you like
this."

Teela took a deep breath and shuddered. "It's him,"
she spat, her face twisting into a scowl.

I raised my eyebrows. "Did he find you?" I asked
frantically.

Teela shook her head. "No, luckily not, but
unfortunately the police haven't found him either."

I frowned. "I'm sure they will find him soon," I
reassured her. "In the meantime, you shouldn't worry about
it. You're safe here with me," I murmured.

Teela dipped her head in gratitude. "I know, Cindy,"
she answered. "I was just lonely by myself today, and
sometimes…" she broke off. "Sometimes I get unpleasant
memories."

I went and sat down next to her on the bed. "I know," I
told her quietly. "It's gonna be alright."

She shook her head bitterly. "I hate that he makes me
so upset like this, it's what he wants!" she spat. "I hate giving
him that satisfaction!" she shuddered again, and her voice
was breaking off. "I remember that night at my house, he kept
peering in the windows… and… ugh… he said… he said that
I'd never be rid of him," she stuttered, trying not to start
sobbing again. "That bloody goddamn bastard," she swore
softly, slamming her hand down on the windowsill.

Even though her face was streaked with tears, I got a
spark when I heard her raspy voice.

"Teela," I murmured. "Please. It's gonna be okay. I
made burritos for dinner when you're ready."

She turned to face me, her hair streaming down her back and her misty moor-grey eyes wide, lips parted breathlessly. She gently brushed a finger over the back of my hand. "Not yet," she whispered, her raspy voice still cloaked with the tears that had streaked her face. Her eyes filled with tears again, and I gently lifted my hands and placed them on her dainty shoulders. I started by rubbing my hands over her shoulders and back lightly, then I began to deeply knead her sore muscles. At first she was stiff beneath my touch, reserved maybe, still upset, but it wasn't long before I felt her relax beneath my hands. She closed her eyes and seemed to melt. Her lips parted slightly and the slightest "ah," slipped between.

"Is this good?" I asked her quietly.

"Oh, yes," she rasped, eyes still closed. Her breath became heavy and she leaned back and arched her back under my hands. Eventually, she turned to face me, and looped her arms around my neck. I simply held her for a while, and then she leaned forward and pressed her lips delicately to mine. Immediately, the flame crackled to life and I threaded my fingers through her wavy black hair, holding her closer. She tasted bittersweet and wonderful, the scent of her lavender body lotion curling around me as she held me. I buried my face in her hair and trailed my lips down the side of her neck. She murmured in approval and her fingers played at the bottom of my lacy shirt. I mirrored her and slid my hands up to peel her shirt away, but she stopped me gently with her hands. The other night we had only kissed but not taken any clothes off.

I pulled back slightly. "Something wrong?" I wondered. "Sorry if I went too far."

Teela shook her head. "It's not your fault," she murmured. "I'm just shy about… something."

"You don't have to be shy," I murmured in return. "It can't be that bad."

"It's all right, Cynthia," she whispered, and lifted her arms. "Go ahead and take my shirt off. Just don't judge me."

I slowly slid her lacy shirt over her head and gasped, for I could see the remnants of what at one time had been nasty black-and blue bruises, now faded to aging scars. I looked her in the eye and knew all at once who had done this to her, and I was filled with a surge of emotion.

"By God, I want to kill that bastard," I bit off, and then my voice softened. "Oh, Teela, I'm so sorry," I murmured, gently rubbing my hands over her back and pressing a kiss to her bare shoulder. She closed her eyes and rested her head on my shoulder, sliding her hands up my shirt. She peeled it over my head and the intensity increased as we lost our clothing very quickly and ended up tangled up on the guest bed with her lying on top of me. Never in my life had I felt as wonderful as the sensation of her hands and lips against my skin. Her skin was burning hot and her hands were skilled, lips were sweet. I knew that she fully trusted me enough to bare her scars, the most sensitive thing about her past. We lost track of the time and our desire flared up so sharply that I thought it might kill me. "God, Teela, you're so beautiful," I murmured as I kissed her scars and I damn near came undone when she whispered my name, giving herself to me.

When we were finally completely breathless and exhausted, we collapsed side-by-side on the bed. "I hope you liked it," I murmured, and she just looked up at me with heavy-lidded eyes.

"Oh, Cynthia," she replied, and I knew that she did. After a while we got our clothes back on.

"It's a damn good thing I didn't start the burritos," I laughed as we were getting dressed. "They would have been charred to a crisp by now."

Teela laughed as well, her eyes twinkling. "I am glad as well," she answered.

We went into the kitchen and she helped me get the burritos together, and I couldn't keep my gaze off of her as she glided around the table, setting our places. Her hair was haphazardly thrown up into a hairclip and her lips were still swollen from our make-out session. I couldn't wait to take her in my arms again.

Chapter Eleven

When I got to work, McGavin continued to act weird all week. "Good morning," he greeted me with a wide smile when I came in.

I tried not to give him a funny look as I put my coat away and got out my work stuff and returned his greeting. What the heck has gotten into him? I thought. Surely there must be a reason that El Groucho suddenly turned into the King of Kindness. Shaking my head, I sat down at my station and logged into my computer.

Teela came to work with me because she had to sign a paper for McGavin, pretty much saying she was done being his client. He had finished all services for her so she was going to pay her final fee and sign a paper. The firm was closing half a day due to bad weather, so it wasn't like Teela had to sit around for hours while I worked. Not that I really could have worked with her there anyway, because she would have inadvertently distracted me beyond belief. McGavin called her in when he said he had time, but I knew by his manner that he had been waiting to call her in just so that he wouldn't seem desperate, or something like that. All thoughts of me being the one he was hitting on vanished when he opened his door.

"Ah, Miss Grant," he greeted her, rubbing his hands together and blatantly looking her up and down. "It's lovely to see you this fine morning. Please do come in."
Teela obliged, greeted him good morning, and stepped into his office. He shut the door most of the way, but due to my strategic seating I could still hear and see what was going on. Okay, yeah, I was really nosey. But I just wanted to see what old McGavin might have up his sleeves. I hoped for Teela's sake that he would just let her sign the paper and leave, but I frankly doubted it. Narrowing my eyes suspiciously, I craned my neck to see in the doorway as McGavin procured the paper for Teela to sign. She handed him the check for the services and read the agreement, then scribbled her signature on the line. She handed the paper back to him and started to depart, but he told her to wait. She turned back to him. "Yes?" she asked.

To my shock, I saw McGavin pull a red rose out from behind his back and present it to her. He bowed low and kissed her hand. "Miss Grant," he intoned. "Now that we are no longer lawyer and client, I wish to pursue you romantically, for you are the most beautiful woman I have ever seen."

While I agreed completely with his statement about her beauty, I saw right through his bullshit act, because I knew that red roses or not, all he wanted was to lay his claim to her body, and I could see it in his eyes, the lecherous gleam that made my flesh crawl with disgust. Damn, I had never known what a creep my boss was.

Most women would have been swooning, but Teela must have agreed with me, because she didn't take the rose. "Thank you for the offer, Attorney," she answered sincerely, a graceful rejection. She spoke so perfectly, so fluently, I could tell that she was a writer. Words were in her blood, and that was one thing I really loved about her. "But I'm afraid I am already romantically involved."

McGavin frowned and took the rose back, still holding it, but he took a defensive stance. "I was not aware of you being in a relationship," he glossed over his obvious chagrin with an even tone of voice.

"Of course," Teela answered, and a smile touched the corner of her mouth. She glanced at me through the door and raised her eyebrows as if to ask permission and I nodded, giving her the go-ahead. "In fact, I am going with your beautiful secretary, Cynthia."

McGavin's mouth opened in shock and he dropped the rose on the floor. "You, a lesbian? And with Cynthia? Surely you are joking," he said evenly. "Such a beautiful woman as you, I wouldn't expect it."

Teela stiffened and took a sharp breath, glaring at him darkly.

He poked his head out. "Are you and Miss Grant in a relationship?" he asked me in a very unprofessional manner, his lips pursing in disgust at the word 'relationship'.

"Yes, we are," I said proudly. Teela winked at me and I beamed.

McGavin retreated back into the office, closing the door most of the way, but I could still hear. "I apologize, Miss Grant, for my unprofessional behavior," he amended. "I did not realize. My congratulations to you and Cynthia."

That was a lame attempt to save your ass, McGavin, I thought. But no smooth talking could undo what he had said. Teela's patience was gone, and I was rooting for her as she delivered the final blow.

"Thank you," Teela bit off briskly, but she looked as if she might kill him. "Now excuse me, Attorney, I believe you are blocking the doorway."

McGavin did nothing but stare as Teela shoved past him. "Good day, Attorney," she finished. He responded by firmly closing his office door, and I heard him curse.

Teela leaned down. "I hope you don't mind that I told him about us," she whispered.

I shook my head. "Of course not," I replied. "I'm so proud that we're together."

Teela nodded. "It takes courage to be public, Cindy," she continued. "But I'm ready."

I nodded. "Me, too," I answered. "Even though our relationship is very new, we have been best friends for quite a while now."

She trailed a finger down the side of my face. "Actually, I'd say it began the day I saw you," she murmured.

I smiled up at her from my chair and squeezed her hand. "Correction," I chuckled. "The day that you nearly blew my brains out. But same here, and if you wanted to kill me, you sure as hell didn't need the gun," I murmured.

Teela coloured, and she looked on me with those beautiful soft eyes of hers, the spark flickering deep within. It took everything in my power not to leap up out of my seat and kiss her freakin' senseless. She must have felt the same, because she stepped back slightly with a small chuckle.

"Too bad we're at work, Cynthia," she murmured. "Because I'd take you up on that offer," she winked. "Don't worry; I'll kill you later."

I sighed. "Mm, sounds good," I replied. "I rather enjoy death. Let's go get some lunch."
Before we headed off down the hallway, I heard McGavin talking on the phone again, in the same low voice as before. And I was unnerved, because it sure as hell didn't sound like a business call. Something was going on, and I feared that Teela and I were involved.

Chapter Twelve

The inclement weather that afternoon was in fact very clement to Teela and me, since we got to go home at noon instead of five o'clock. I had a lot of housework to do, just straightening up, and I of course had to take Butler out, even though it was below zero. He did his business quickly, then came bounding right back in with his tail between his legs. The wind was whipping around at gusts up to fifteen miles an hour, hurling snow across the barren, desolate landscape. I looked out the window around four o'clock and it was already beginning to get dark around the edges of the sky, no visible sign of life in the howling snowdrift outside. Grateful to be inside out of the cold, I cranked up the furnace and Butler lay down in front of the heating grate, warming himself. Teela was working on her manuscript and I was tidying up the kitchen, making preparations for cooking and absentmindedly listening to the radio. I loved reading cookbooks, even if I wouldn't cook or eat many of the dishes. For some reason, I just found it comforting to look at the checkered cover of the cookbook and flip through the pages and pages of crispy appetizers and delectable desserts. *Hmm, I'll make something special this weekend,* I mused. I was listening to the radio and crunching on a peppermint. Damn, I was so addicted to those things. I always got thinking about something and never sucked on them like a normal person, but crunched down with vigor, my lips pursed in concentration. Candy canes, on the other hand, were a totally different story. I sucked on candy canes like my life depended on it, licking and tasting every bit. Don't ask me why, it was just a quirk. Anyway, I was looking at a recipe but not really reading it, leaning over the counter and gazing off into space. I bobbed my head to the next song on the radio. I was off in my own world, until something soft and silky and dark covered my eyes. At first I was slightly alarmed, but then I smelled lavender and knew it was Teela.

"Teela Grant," I murmured. "How did I know it was you?"

Teela leaned in until her lips were brushing my neck. "I made you a promise earlier, Cynthia," she rasped. "And I've been waiting all day to fulfill it."

I remembered what she had said to me earlier, and I shivered with anticipation. I was cold, and all I wanted was her hands on me. "Why do you have me blindfolded?" I asked her.

"Surprise," Teela replied softly and she suddenly, swiftly spun me around and took me in her arms, crushing her pretty mouth to mine. "You taste so good, Cynthia," she whispered. "Peppermint."

I flicked my tongue around her lips, tasting her lip lacquer that somewhat resembled the taste of brandy. She parted my lips and flicked her tongue into my mouth, and I let her in, murmuring and lacing my fingers through her hair, despite the somewhat cumbersome blindfold. I sort of wished that she would take it off but it was somehow thrilling to be blinded, completely at her mercy.

I was still blindfolded as she took me down the hall and she gently pushed me back on the bed. "May I take your shirt off, Cynthia?" Teela murmured, her fingers playing along the hem of my lacy shirt.

I lifted my arms. "Be my guest," I replied, and she slid her palms up my sides and peeled my shirt over my head, then offered me the chance to return the favor. We kissed some more and lost the rest of our clothes, and when I reached up to touch her face I found that she was blindfolded too.

"You're blindfolded too?" I asked in disbelief.

"Yes," she answered. "I don't need to see to feel your beauty."

Blindfolded and with only two mere scraps of fabric preventing us from being completely nude, leopard-print cotton in my case and black lace in her case, I pulled her down on top of me and we blindly learned each other's shapes with our hands and tongues until we finally wore ourselves out and gently lifted each other's blindfolds off. Teela looked at me with a twinkle in her eye. "What did you think?" she whispered. "Did you like my surprise?"

I beamed at her. "I loved it, Teela," I replied. "How did you manage to stay so steady with that blindfold on?" I wondered.

She winked. "Oh, I just feel my way," she tossed off, grinning at me. I laughed but a bolt of raw lightning shot straight through me.

"Yeah, you certainly do, Teela Grant," I replied, studying her with coy eyes and running a finger over my lip. She smiled sultrily and gently grasped my chin, closing her eyes and preparing to kiss me again, but we were interrupted by a banging on the door. "Open up! Police!" came the sharp voice.

"Shit," Teela and I swore almost simultaneously, scrambling for our clothes. "Just a second!" Teela shouted. We sat bolt up and jammed our clothes on as fast as we could, neglecting bras and I ended up with my shirt on backwards, but we didn't care. I hastened to the door and looked out the peephole, since it was my house. I saw a guy in a coat and wool hat, and he flashed some sort of badge. I disengaged the lock and thrust the door open, hands on my hips.

"Yes?" I inquired, sort of annoyed at having my make-out with Teela interrupted, but then again, if they had any news about Teela's psychotic ex, I would be grateful. I didn't think much of this detective already, though; he was shifty-eyed and spoke in a sort of whiny voice.

"I'm Detective Barstow," the man explained. "We have some information about a certain suspect. Is Miss Teela Grant at home? I was told that she lives here."

I looked at him suspiciously. "Detective, could I see your credentials again?" I asked him.

"Sure," he answered affably, but instead of pulling out his badge, he drew a pistol and pointed it at me, then he whipped off his hat and his bald head gleamed in the light of my porch light. It was Frank! "So you're the faggot that has my woman," he spat.

Teela came out from the other room at the sound of the commotion. When she saw Frank, her face was stricken with horror.

"No!" I shouted. "Teela, stay back!"

Quickly, I slammed and locked the door. I could hear him pounding but I barred it and put as heavy chair in front of it.

"Call the police," I whispered to Teela. She ran into the other room and picked up the phone, began dialing.

Teela had just connected with the 911 operator when there was a tremendous crash in the living room, followed by the sound of splintering glass. I told Teela to hide in the closet and lock the door while she talked to 911, and I went to investigate. Just as I had feared, Frank had swung a crowbar and splintered my window. He pointed his pistol in again, and his creepy face leered through the shattered glass. "Hey, fag," he called. "I'll make a deal with you."

The only good thing about stalling him was that he could be caught when the police showed up. I prayed that they showed up soon. "Here's the deal," he continued, keeping his revolver trained on me. "We can do this one of two ways. One. You will let me take Teela, and I will let you alone. Or Two..." he held up a second finger. "I can kill you, then I will do what I please with your lovely Teela," he laughed maniacally and rubbed his hands together.

"You will not take Teela," I spat. "And I am not afraid of you, you sick bastard."

Frank rubbed his hands together. "Very well," he pretended to consider. "I hate to shoot a pretty young lady such as yourself; but I swear to God, I will once again be in control of Teela Grant!" He lifted a fist to the sky. "She ran from me once, but she will not run again. I will make it so she will never run from me again."

He leveled his pistol and clicked the safety off, and I looked around for something to divert him with. I could run out of the room, I thought, but he could very well climb in the window and shoot up the house, and I didn't want Teela to get hurt. "Just let me say my last prayer," I told him, and I bowed my head.

He seemed to be thrown off, because he lowered his gun. My prayer must have been answered because just then, the adjoining door burst open and Teela came barreling out, brandishing a heavy piece of lumber.

"Teela!" I shrieked, and Frank fired a shot, but it simply whistled through the room and smashed clean through the window on the other side.

He grabbed his gun to aim again but before he could readjust his aim, Teela cursed and swung the beam at him, knocking the gun successfully out of his hand. She must have swung a little too hard, because the board connected soundly with his nose with a sickening crack and he fell back into the snow. "Bastard!" she ranted, and I could see the years of hurt in her eyes, all the times that he had beat her like that, all of those bruises and scars all over her beautiful body. Poor Teela. I didn't care if the goddamn bastard froze to death, he deserved it, I thought. Teela suddenly cast the wooden bar aside and sank down onto the floor, sobbing her heart out. She cried and yelled in pain and misery, and I held her in my arms, whispering "shh, it's okay," and rubbing her back. She was curled up with her head in my lap like a baby and her sobs were just beginning to dwindle into hiccups when the doorbell rang. I went to the door and knew it couldn't be Frank, but I double-checked just in case. There were two police cars out front and an ambulance on the way. The man at the door showed all of his credentials and introduced himself as Officer Doolin. He asked me what had happened and I told him to the best of my ability in brief. He said that Teela and I would have to testify in court at a later date, but this was just the basics. He pointed out the door where EMT's were loading Frank onto a gurney. He had suffered a broken nose and frostbite and was currently unconscious, Officer Doolin said. I was worried that Teela's swing at Frank with the board might count against her, but Doolin reassured me that it was an act of self-defense so it wouldn't even be an issue. "No one is going to prosecute that poor woman," he told me.

When they had finished and the EMT's took Frank away, I closed the door and made a pot of coffee for Teela and myself. She was still upset and shaken, her face haggard and tear-stained. I did my best to calm her down, and after a while she did, just sitting and sipping her coffee. She didn't speak for the longest time, but finally she did.

"I'm just glad that he's gone, Cindy."

"Me, too, Teela," I answered. "Me, too."

The immediate crisis was over but I could see in her eyes that the scars remained.

Chapter Thirteen

When I got to work a few days later, I was late of course, having overslept through my alarm. When I finally did arrive, I was baffled to see McGavin and the manager of the place, Mr. McPherson, standing in front of my desk. McGavin glanced at his watch and frowned, then turned to McPherson, nodding. McPherson mumbled, "I'll handle this," and motioned McGavin back to his office, which gave me a sour look but complied. What the hell? I thought, since McGavin had been so nice to me the other day. I had known that something was fishy when he started acting like that.

"Good morning, Mr. McPherson," I chirped, trying to save face. Something about his stern expression told me trouble might be on the way.

"Good morning, Miss Washek," he returned. "Will you please follow me into my office? We have something to discuss, I believe."
He turned on his heel and I followed him into his spacious office. He motioned me to take a seat in the client chair and he promptly shut the door with a smart clack.

"What seems to be the matter?" I asked him as he walked around his desk and took a seat. Sighing, he folded his hands.

"I really hate to do this to you, Cynthia," he began, "but unfortunately your boss, Jim McGavin, thinks that your work ethic is inadequate and needs improvement."

"I'm sorry I was late," I told him. "I've had a lot going on lately."

McPherson nodded, stroking his chin. "I gather that, but unfortunately being late isn't the attorney's only concern. To be frank with you, your employment is in jeopardy."

I leaned forward and gasped. "What?" I asked, and my brow furrowed. "You mean I'm fired?"

McPherson inhaled sharply. "If Mr. McGavin had his way, then yes. But I've reconsidered and decided to give you a chance. I know that you are a good worker, but your performance needs to improve within the next two weeks or your employment is terminated. Capisce?"

I nodded. "Okay, Mr. McPherson, thank you," I replied.

He nodded. "We'd hate to lose you, Miss Washek. Mr. McGavin was very upset with your work, though. I'd watch my back if I were you. Have a good day," he stood opened the door.

"You as well," I answered, and departed.

The only possible reason for this sudden complaint would be something to do with Teela, and perhaps that sinister phone call that McGavin had made the other day. I shook my head and headed back up to my desk. I knocked on McGavin's door, and he called out for me to enter.

"What is the exact complaint you have with me, Mr. McGavin?" I asked, trying to be polite. "If you let me know, I will improve."

He shook his head, disgruntled. "Your work is shoddy, Miss Washek," he answered. "No further explanation needed."

I bowed my head, trying to look pensive and like I was contemplating how to improve my career. "Okay, well, I will try to improve," I told him.

He didn't even bother to look up from his desk. "I hope so," he answered. "Why don't you go do it now?"

***

The rest of the day went by pretty seamlessly, sort of uneventfully. I was stressed out about the fact that I might lose my job, and so I was on the edge all day long. When it came around to near quitting time, I realized that damn; I could really use a treat of some kind. I had worked with almost straining concentration and my brow had been furrowed in aggravated intent all day long.

Looking at the clock, I breathed a sigh of relief when I saw the readout as two minutes to five. I started packing up my stuff and put my coat on, slinging my bag over my shoulder. On the way out, I waved goodbye to McGavin, who was slightly disgruntled but gave a muffled grunt as a makeshift farewell, which was typical. I decided that I would stop at the Townhouse Café on the way home and pick up a hot chocolate or cappuccino for myself and I decided to get one for Teela as well, as a little treat. In the parking lot of the Townhouse, which wasn't too far from the firm, I called Teela and told her that I'd be a few minutes late. She told me in her soft, quiet voice that I could take all the time I needed, but that she'd miss me and be waiting for me at home. I blew her a kiss and hung up, bundling up my coat to brave the cold outside.

I hurried to the door with my head down and pulled it open, immediately greeted with the spicy-sweet scent of coffee and chocolate carried on an inviting warm wind. Inside, the Townhouse had a high ceiling, vaulted, with chandeliers, cozy tables, and a big bar and drink counter with a menu posted on the wall. It was a real swanky place, and they served almost any type of hot or cold drink that one could dream of, and also small snacks like hot cinnamon rolls, cookies, cakes, etc. all hand baked. It was extremely expensive but the lead chef was one of the top three chefs in town, so it was worth the exorbitant cost. No one made coffee, lattes, hot chocolate or cinnamon rolls as heavenly as this chef did.

I headed in and looked around, taking a deep appreciative sniff of the fragrant air. I strode up to the bar counter and unfortunately, there was a slight line. I waited behind someone else, and then when they were done, I stepped up to the counter.

The guy behind the counter greeted me and asked for my order.

"Two cappuccinos and two cinnamon rolls, please," I said automatically.

He told me what the price was and I fished through my wallet. I waited while they processed my order, and looked up when I saw a slightly familiar guy bringing a bag and two cups in a drink holder. He was blond with blue eyes, not too tall but on the skinny-buff line. He wore glasses perched on the bridge of his nose and he had a tattoo peeking out from beneath the scoop of his shirt, and another one on his wrist. I didn't pay too much attention to him, took my order, and was about to leave when he called after me.

"Hey, Cindy," he called.

I whipped around, stunned. "I know you from somewhere," I told him. "But I can't remember your name."

He grinned at me, revealing a row of beautiful white teeth, but not too unnaturally white. "Surely you remember me," he chuckled. "I was just the neighborhood math nerd in your high school class."

My mouth dropped open but no words came out. No, it couldn't be him. Not here. Billy Lynn Kramer was a virtual genius at math and engineering, taking college classes at age fifteen. We had always been friends, and I had always sort of admired his math ability from afar. He was not a geek to the other kids, they sort of just held him off in a class all of his own. We had always had kind of a weird friendship, but for some reason we never dated.

"Billy Lynn Kramer," I replied. "It's you. When did you get tatted up?"

Billy grinned and rolled up his sleeve. "Last summer," he informed me proudly. "Two of 'em."

We moved to the side to keep talking, and the other guy took over taking orders. "Did it hurt?" I asked incredulously.

Instead of lying and trying to play tough, Billy just nodded. "Shit, yeah, it did," he answered truthfully. "Like hell freezing over. But it was worth it."

"I bet," I answered. "So what is a mathematical genius like you doing working at a coffee shop?" I wondered.

He shrugged. "I'm working on my master's degree, then hopefully my PHD in engineering. I have time off and I am trying to defray costs."

I nodded. "Ah, I see," I answered. "That makes perfect sense."

Billy and I caught up and chatted for a while before I told him that I should get going.

"You gonna drink both of those?" he joked, referring to the cups of cappuccino. I shook my head.

"Nah, I'm taking one home with me," I answered, which was true, but I didn't exactly feel like telling him about Teela quite yet.

"That's too bad," he answered, mock pouting. "I thought one was for me."

I chuckled, not sure if to be flattered or annoyed. I decided to bite the bullet and tell him.
"Sorry, Billy, it's for my girlfriend," I told him.

His jaw dropped. "Jesus Christ, Cindy, you're a lesbian?" he burst out. Several people around us glanced over with curious stares. Embarrassed, Billy flushed then he lowered his voice. "God, I'm sorry," he apologized. "I didn't mean to sound like that. It just shocked me, that's all."

I nodded. "Yeah, it shocks a lot of people," I told him. "But yeah, I am."

He studied me for a moment. "This is new, isn't it?" he wondered.

I shrugged. "Yeah, pretty new," I told him. "Teela and I only got together a while ago."

"Teela, huh?" Billy responded. "Well listen, Cindy, you and Teela take care tonight. It was nice to see you."

"Nice to see you too, Billy," I answered, and I turned to leave. "My cappuccino is getting cold, sorry."

Billy grinned and waved, but before I was out of earshot he called after me again. "Hope I see you again, Cindy." His words lingered in the air as I opened the door and was slapped by the icy wind.

When I got into my car, I was shivering, so I turned on the heat and the radio. My eyes were sort of bleary from the snow and ice, and it was starting to get dark. I hoped that our drinks weren't getting cold, I thought to myself as I turned on the blower.

The driving conditions were abominable on the way home, and I was going about two miles per hour and could barely see. Funny that I would run into Billy Lynn Kramer, I thought, him of all people. He had been the valedictorian of our class and now he was working at a coffee shop. Life has a funny way of tossing in unexpected twists, I guessed. Yeah, admittedly, I had had a small crush on him in high school but that was over now. I swerved, sliding slightly and nearly colliding with another car. Shaken, I took a deep breath, my knuckles still white on the steering wheel. Damn, I hated driving in January, especially when it was cold and dangerous conditions like this. I turned the wipers on a higher setting and they did their best to clear away the flurries of snow that were furiously landing against my windshield. Finally, I breathed a sigh of relief when I spotted my street, and I pulled up to my house and parked in the driveway. As I stepped out of the car, I was overcome with a wash of gratitude when I saw that Teela had shoveled the sidewalk and brushed off the steps. Gad, she was wonderful. My house never looked as good as it did when she was around, because she was very skilled at cleaning and took the time to clean while she was taking a break from writing her books while I was at work. I walked up the shoveled path to my door, and I pulled out my key, twisting it in the lock.

When I got inside, Teela was sitting on the sofa, working on her manuscript. She had her glasses perched on the bridge on her nose and was focused intently on her work, her black hair pulled up in a hairclip with some assorted capped and uncapped pens sticking out at odd angles. Teela was slightly eccentric, and something like the uncapped pens in her hair just made me smile. She was wearing a camo-patterned scoop-neck shirt with an edgy black lace neckline and black leggings that clung to her thin legs. As usual, her feet were bare and her legs were crossed, even though she was sitting on the couch. She didn't even notice that I had come in, since she was so absorbed in her work, scribbling away, her lips parted slightly. I studied her for a second from the other room, all thoughts of Billy Kramer vanishing like the wind as I watched her write. I hung up my coat in the closet and took all of my outerwear off, and then I headed into the room.

"Hey, Teela, I'm home," I announced.
She glanced up and smiled at me, setting her pen down to return my greeting.
"I brought us a surprise," I continued, taking out the tray with the cappuccinos and cinnamon rolls. "Sorry, it might be a little cold."

"I bet it will be just fine," Teela answered. "Thanks, Cindy."

I grinned as I handed over her cup. "I know how much you love the townhouse cappuccino," I told her.

She beamed at me, and lowered her eyes. Dang, I thought. It was one of those times when she was really hot to me. I sat down next to her on the couch and took a sip of my cappuccino. When I set it down on the table, I took her hand. We sat in silence for a while, enjoying our treat. As she held my hand, I loved the way she stroked my fingers and my wrist, almost massaging my hand. Her sprite-like fingers

flicked lightly over my skin, tracing my veins, and I shivered with pleasure. I loved when she did that, and she knew it.
"I got a little delayed," I explained. "The traffic was slow."

Teela took a sip of her drink. "Don't worry about it," she murmured, glancing at me sideways and squeezing my hand lightly.

I looked down at the cinnamon rolls and saw that hers had chocolate glaze while mine had vanilla glaze. "Mm, chocolate," I sighed guiltily. "Do you mind if I have a piece?"

Teela studied me. "Of course not," she replied with a sly grin. She pinched off a piece and lifted it to my lips. I took it gratefully, and she 'accidentally' smeared chocolate glaze on my face. "Whoops," she lied.

I threw my head back and laughed. "Oh no, you don't," I countered, and smeared a swatch of vanilla around her lips. She smiled and licked it off.

"Delicious," she murmured, smacking her lips together. We laughed and continued to smear each other with frosting until it was completely smeared all over our lips. I was floored by how pretty she looked and I took her hand.

"Come here, you," I murmured, and she twined her arms around my neck and closed her eyes, trailing a fingertip down my cheek. I leaned back on the couch, pulling her down on top of me and she flicked her tongue around my mouth, sucking the frosting off my lips. By now we were an absolutely sticky mess but didn't care. I always missed her when I was at work, and I loved feeling her figure molded to mine on the couch, her black inky hair falling all around my face.

When we had broken apart, she asked me how my day was, and I told her that I had nearly gotten fired. I also told her my suspicions about McGavin's sinister behavior.

She nodded gravely. "You should investigate," she told me.
"I can't," I gasped. "I'm not allowed in his office when he isn't there."

Teela threaded her long, thin fingers together and rested her chin on her hands, thinking.

"Well, it would be a risk you would be taking," she continued. "But you might not have a choice in the matter. He will find a way to oust you if you don't oust him first."

The direness of Teela's words sank in with bone-chilling clarity, and I knew the truth. It would have to be a battle of the wits, Jim McGavin against Cynthia Washek. If he caught me searching his office, I was toast. If I did nothing, I was toast, and finally, if I was successful, I was possibly still toast. I shook my head. "Don't wanna think about that tonight," I told her, and I shuddered. I had a slight suspicion that McGavin might have been involved in setting up Frank's midnight visit the other night, since he was the only one who knew at the time that Teela was staying at my house. It would be dangerous, but I figured he was up to something, and maybe out to get me or Teela. I had to do something about it. If I did it wrong, it would cost me.

Teela leaned over. "Listen, Cynthia, don't worry about that tonight," she murmured against my lips.

Chapter Fourteen

The next day I wore an innocent expression and a professional-looking charcoal grey skirt, but I had a plan. I was looking for the opportunity that I could search McGavin's office. I eventually decided to search it while he was at lunch. In the meantime, I worked sweetly and focused on everything that I was supposed to do. I was pleasant to McGavin, but not overly pleasant, so that he wouldn't suspect anything of me. He paid me no extra mind, only gave me his usual orders to get things done. I found it strange that his door was always closed. Most of the lawyers left their doors at least partway open and shut their doors only when they were on the phone. McGavin, however, always kept his door shut and locked it even when he got up to get coffee. One of two things was going on. Either he was doing something suspicious, or he was just a really private guy. I had a suspicion that he had something to do with Teela or me, and Teela and I had agreed that I should check it out. I wasn't sure what I might find, or not find, but it was worth a try. It would be an extremely dangerous mission, though, because I had absolutely no idea whatsoever where to start. It seemed to take forever until lunchtime, and I waited while McGavin picked up his stuff and prepared to head off to lunch. Finally, he took his wallet and locked his office door, heading off down the hall. Shit, I thought to myself. I knew that he would lock the door. I put my head in my hands. Damn, there was no way in hell that I could go through with this now. I was stumped, but only for a moment. I knew someone who would have the key to McGavin's office. With new energy, I headed down the hall to the maintenance room, which was really more of a broom closet. The janitor, Pete, was sitting in there and eating his lunch. I knew I could trust Pete not to squeal on me.

"Hiya, there, Cindy," he drawled in his thick southern accent. He was quite a hillbilly, but he was a sweet guy. "What can I do for ya?"

"Hey, Pete," I responded, trying to sound casual. "Listen, I've got a file due for Atty. McGavin in an hour and he might not be back from lunch by then. Would you happen to have the key to his office?"

Pete didn't even think twice, and I knew he wouldn't. "Just a moment," he answered, riffling through his key chain. Finally, he selected the right key and handed it to me. "This is it, Miss Cindy," he answered. I took it with gratitude.

"Thanks, Pete," I answered. "I'll bring this back after lunch."

Pete took a bite of his tuna roll. "Sure thing," he replied, paying me no mind as I exited his closet-office. It was an absolutely natural thing for a secretary to ask for the key to her boss's office, and I was thankful for all of the free-reign that secretaries were awarded.

I slipped back down the nearly empty corridor, grateful that almost everyone was at lunch. I slipped the key in the lock and creaked the door open. Immediately, I was hit with a foreboding wave of his aftershave, and felt creeped out, as if his phantom presence was recording my every move. I eased the door shut and snuck over to his desk. Act natural, I told myself. My palms were sweating, but I took a deep breath and began to riffle through all of the papers on his desk. Nope, nothing yet. Lots of cases and papers, briefs, dates, post-its, etc. I was about ready to give up, when I spied a small folded sheet of paper under his keyboard. "Username: MCGAVIN, Password: packers2" it read. Hmm, I thought. Maybe this was it. The online filing database! I logged onto his computer, checking over my shoulder, but no one was coming. His computer account was open so I opened the database and was confronted with the login screen. I deftly entered the information, praying that it was right. The little icon loaded for a few seconds, and I breathed "come on, come on," until finally with a soft click, I was in.

Inside the virtual filing cabinet, there were hundreds and hundreds of files. I quickly found that they were sorted by last name. It would be a good start to search Teela's file, I thought, and I searched for "Grant". A little window popped up that said "File does not exist."

Shit, I muttered, and began to retrace my steps when I looked at McGavin's recent activity. I saw a file labeled TG14412 and I thought to open it. TG, I thought. Teela Grant, maybe?

I clicked on the file and another window popped up, asking me to retype my password for confirmation. "Private file" it read. "Please confirm password."
Taking a deep breath, I reentered McGavin's password and it accepted. I opened up the TG14412 file and found at first that it was just a bunch of garbled nonsense. But when I adjusted the monitor, I saw that it was a spreadsheet. It had a date line and some more scribbles, followed by what seemed like a word-for-word documentation of a conversation, followed by meticulous notes with some underlining and highlighting. Halfway down the page, I caught the word "Grant" and the word "ex-husband" and I knew that it was Teela's case. My mouth dropped open in shock. McGavin was recording word-for-word all of his conversations with Teela and analyzing them, taking notes on what she said. Damn, what a creep, I thought. Wait till she gets a load of this. I was about to hit print when I heard his voice down the hall, coming closer.

Shit, I thought. He would hang me up to dry if he found me here, and my entire plan would be ruined. I could be fired immediately, or worse. Scrambling and entering panic mode, I whacked the print button and closed the files, trying to leave them the way they were, shutting down his computer. I tried to quickly rearrange his files on his desk the way he had them.

I heard his voice and he sounded awfully close. I grabbed the pages off the printer and peered out the crack of the door. Luckily, his back was turned and he was talking to someone else. Maybe if I was quiet, I could slip out behind his back. Walking on eggshells, I slipped out the door and quietly pulled it shut behind me, and then I ran across the hall. I plopped down in my chair, flushed and clutching my evidence, just as the wind blew the door all the way shut and the lock clicked loudly into place. McGavin whipped around to see what the source of the noise was, but I sat there nonchalantly typing away, free of blame. In a few seconds he lost interest and finished up his conversation. "Back from lunch early, Mr. McGavin?" I asked him as he twirled the key in his lock.

He shot me something between a stare and a glare. "Yes, I am," he replied. "Did you work through lunch today, Miss Washek?"

I shook my head. "Nah, grabbed something to eat first," I lied. "I just wanted to get some things done."

He gave a nod. "Good," he answered, and abruptly closed his door behind him. As long as he wasn't being freakishly nice, I thought, everything was ok for now. I surreptitiously stuffed my findings into my purse, half folded and half crumpled, once McGavin had gone into his office.

***

Later that day when I headed home from work, my mind was on the sinister documents that I had printed off from McGavin's computer. There had to be a reason that he was watching and documenting Teela's every move. Why, I wasn't entirely sure but I had my suspicions. I bumbled in through the back door into the dark rear part of the house, tossing my keys on the table and going to hang up my coat. There was not much light coming from the house, only a dim gleam from the kitchen or living room, and the fresh, garlic aroma of stew threaded through the warm air. I was so grateful to Teela for making dinner, and besides her chili lentil stew was top-of-the-line, no question about it. I headed into the kitchen, where she was stirring the pot of stew, looking pensively at a spot on the wall, as she often did when she was thinking. She looked up when she saw me coming.

"Hi, Teela," I greeted her.

"Hey there," she replied, her lips drawn up in her signature pinch of a smile, her eyes crinkling kindly.

I set my bag down on the floor. "How was your day?" I asked her, waiting to tell her about the papers.

She shrugged. "It was pretty good," she answered. "I'm almost done with my novel. I'm just glad to be rid of you-know-who. Say, speaking of, did you find anything in McGavin's office?"

I nodded, stern-faced. "Yes, as a matter of a fact I did. Wait till you get a load of what I found. Come in the other room and I will show it to you."

Teela grimaced. "Doesn't sound good, Cindy," she replied.

"It isn't good," I confirmed. "McGavin's up to something."

She followed me into the other room and we sat down on the tan couch. I opened up my folder that contained the sheaf of forbidden papers and I pulled them out. The top sheet read with the file number. I handed the papers to Teela and she started to flip through. The first paper or so was just general case stuff, normal things to be in a divorce case, nothing out of the ordinary. But then came the page with the dates and times at the top, and dialogue recorded and printed out. Teela's mouth dropped open in shock and outrage as her eyes skimmed over the page. "That bastard!" she burst out. "He was writing down everything I ever said to him."

There was an entire fact sheet on Teela as well as special notes of when she would be home, wouldn't be home, etc. "Why would McGavin do that?" I asked her.

We speculated for a while then found a phone number on a sticky note attached to the page. "That's Frank's number," Teela pointed out, shocked.

Suddenly it all clicked. "That's it!" I exclaimed. "McGavin collected all of this information and then relayed it to Frank. He had me as his secretary and all of your personal information as his client, so it was a piece of cake."

Teela frowned. "That would certainly explain how Frank found us," she answered. "But I wonder what McGavin is getting out of all of this... he certainly wouldn't provide all of that information for free, at risk of confidentiality breaching."

I nodded, finger to my temple. "Very true," I answered. We searched the document for evidence of another piece of the puzzle, but we could find nothing that indicated otherwise.

Finally, Teela's fingertip came to rest on a single line and her mouth dropped open again. "I never told him that I broke my hip," she looked up at me, her eyes wide. "And I don't think he has access to my medical records."

"Hm," I replied. "I don't know."
It was fishy, but not too fishy to warrant much further explanation. Then we came upon a diagram of Teela's house, showing an x-ray view of the inside, same with my house. What the fuck was going on?

"This is unbelievable," Teela exclaimed. "What are we going to do next?"

I drew a deep breath. "Well, I'll start by figuring out why McGavin has all of this information on you and if it has anything to do with your ex."

Teela nodded. "Sounds like a good start," she answered. "Also, let's try to find out how he got the information."

I made a note. "Good call," I muttered. We had a mission on our hands. "Well, we have quite a bit of progress already, just finding these things and tying it to Frank," I told her.

Teela agreed. "I'm glad we got this far, but a lot could still be going on." She shuddered. "I hope we're safe."

I nodded. "Me, too," I agreed uneasily. I looked out the window and could barely make out the shadow of a figure slipping off down the street, seemingly coming from our property. "A spy," I gasped. "Someone is watching our house."

"Let's get a security light," Teela suggested. "A huge, beaming spotlight."

I frowned and nodded. "That might work," I answered. We discussed it for a while until we decided that the best we could do for tonight was to lock all of the doors and windows and to keep the lights as low as possible. Teela and I enjoyed a candlelit dinner, it was a great way to keep the lights low, and soon the troubles drifted toward the back of my mind when I saw my girlfriend's beautiful face in the candle light across the table from me. We both reached for the salad spoon at the same time and our fingers brushed. I was lit with an electric pulse just like the first time I touched her, and she smiled and squeezed my hand. The table was small and our feet were very close to each other. We both had our shoes off, and she wore mismatched polka-dot and striped socks, and I wore green monster socks. One thing Teela and I really both loved was crazy socks, and we often tried to determine whose socks were cooler but never could.

"I'm afraid for you, Teela," I said to her, my hands folded on the table. All of this business was really bothering me and it was still dampening the mood.

Teela nodded. "I am, too," she answered softly, pensively. "But on the other hand, we could die tomorrow and it wouldn't matter."

I furrowed my brow, "True…" I started, but she cut me off.

"So let's not let the time we have go to waste, Cynthia," she murmured, and before I knew it, her sock-clad foot was sliding up my leg under the table.

I gasped and turned a little red at her bold move. My whole body heated up as her dainty foot made its incline and my face flamed crimson when she traced her toe around the tops of my thighs. I couldn't look at her across the table.

"God, Teela," I muttered, but then my mortified grumble turned into a breathy murmur as she continued, all the while studying me with those piercing, misty eyes of hers. I stumbled and spilled coffee down my shirt. I got up to get a paper towel to dab up the mess but Teela was up and out of her chair with a flash. I was in the kitchen and she was dabbing at the stain, her lips pursed in concentration. When the stain was relatively dry and she was about to go back to the table, I grabbed her wrist. "Teela," I murmured, and she threw her arms around my neck, slammed me up against the counter and crushed her glossy, peppermint-flavored lips to mine. I plowed my fingers through her hair and we got distracted from cleaning up the dishes, the cluttered table forgotten as her tongue flicked in and out of my mouth with the grace of a hummingbird.

I was gasping for breath and her hands were trailing up my bare back when we noticed a strange glow and broke apart. "Holy shit!" I yelled, and rushed, topless, into the dining room. In the breathless fit of our passion, we had left the candle unattended and it had tipped. Luckily, there was only a small flame, but we rushed anyway. I grabbed a pail of water and Teela began beating it out as I doused it. The tablecloth was charred, but luckily, nothing else was damaged. It took a while to smother the last sparks and embers but we breathed a sigh of relief when the last spark died out and Teela balled up the charred, wet, and ruined tablecloth and stuffed it in the trash.

"Wow, you're so hot you almost burned the house down," I joked to Teela once the crisis was over.

Instead of rolling her eyes at my lame pun, Teela's lips curved into a smile. "Shall I try again, Cynthia?" she murmured, sliding her hands over my hips.

I looped my arms around her neck and we headed to the living room. "Yes," I murmured in return. "Oh, yes, Teela."

We dissolved into each other's arms, but the threat of the unknown conspiracy still hung in the air like a blanket of smog.

Chapter Fifteen

The next day, I was in a funk, plain and simple. The threat of McGavin's mystery still hung over my head disturbingly. I was floating aimlessly down the corridors of my semi-soporific mind when I was awakened by a persistent "beep, BEEP... beep, BEEP..."

"Aw, damn," I muttered, swiping at my alarm clock on my nightstand. The readout confirmed my chagrin; it was time to get up for work. I turned on my bedside lamp and the bright light speared into my bleary eyes with almost painful intensity. Grumbling and rubbing my eyes with irritation, I staggered out of bed, almost comatose from lack of sleep the last few nights. I stumbled into the bathroom, brushed my teeth, and hopped into the shower.

When I had gotten dressed and headed into the kitchen to fix myself some breakfast, I was surprised that Teela was nowhere to be seen. I poured my coffee then ventured into the other room to look for her. It didn't take me very long to find Teela; she was sitting on the couch, reading the paper. Her eyes were focused intently on the print and she didn't look up. I wasn't sure if she knew I was there or not, but she seemed to be kind of closed off.

"Morning, Teela," I greeted her, coffee cup in hand.

She looked up finally, her moor-grey eyes misty and unreadable. I wasn't quite sure what I saw flickering behind her eyes, but it hit me like a tidal wave. I could see the scars and lacerations that marred her soul. Frank's physical abuse was evident in the faded bruises that covered Teela's shoulders and left their stain on her frail skin, but the extent of her emotional injuries was far more colossal. "Morning, Cindy," she answered softly.

I sat down next to her on the couch and put my arm around her. "What's wrong?" I murmured.

"I'm fine," Teela answered blithely, but I knew that it was a complete lie. "Just a little tired, that's all."

I rubbed her shoulders. "Oh, Teela," I murmured. "Listen, if you want me to help, just let me know."

She surprised me by simply gently shrugging off my arm and rising from the couch. "Okay," she answered. "Have a good work day."

"Teela…" I began, but I didn't even get to continue because her reply was the door gently but firmly closing in my face.

I shrugged my shoulders, feeling my heart pricked like a deflated balloon as I wrestled my winter coat on and headed out the door. "Hope you feel better!" I called as I was leaving. She did not reply.

Later, as I was sitting at my desk, I felt just sort of lost and crapped out. I knew that Teela wasn't trying to be mean this morning, but it hurt so badly when she shut me out like that. I thought about calling her, but then I got busy so I didn't. I began to wonder whether she really trusted me or not. Maybe she didn't. McGavin seemed very subdued, and if he knew about my little sleuthing adventure in his office, he certainly didn't show it. Lunchtime rolled around and I wasn't even hungry, so instead I just lay my head down on my desk, hoping to catch an hour of z's before I had to get back to work. I had just started to slightly drift off when I was jarred by the shrill ringing of my desk phone. Thinking, hoping, it might be Teela, I picked it up without surveying the number. "This is Cindy," I answered.

I was not prepared for the mellow male voice that flowed through the speakers. "Hey, Cindy, it's me, Billy Kramer from the coffee shop," the voice began.

I sat up. "Hi, Billy," I answered. "I'm surprised you called. Do you need legal services? Because my boss is at lunch."

Billy laughed quietly, musically. "No, Cindy," he answered. "I called to talk to you. Listen, it's my lunch break too, so I could come pick you up and take you to lunch. Whaddaya say?"

I considered. I didn't want Billy to get the wrong idea, but on the other hand, I could use a break from the office. Finally, I answered. I took a deep breath. "Sure, why not," I answered.

Billy blew out a sigh of relief. "Great!" he chirped. "I'll be there in about three minutes, see you soon!"

"Yup, see you," I answered, and set the phone down. I picked up my coat and headed out to the lobby where I sat down in one of the chairs to wait for Billy to arrive. Anna, the receptionist, smiled at me. "Got a lunch date, huh, Cindy?" she asked, looking up from her keyboard.

I shrugged. "It's not a date," I answered. "A friend invited me out to lunch."

"Male friend?" Anna wondered. I said yes.

"Is he cute?" she continued. She didn't know about me and Teela.

"Ah…" I began, not sure what to tell her. "Maybe a little."

She smiled. "Cool," she replied. "Tell him that Anna at the front desk says hi."

I chuckled. "Okay, I will," I answered with a smile. Anna was a little bit older than me, and always flirted with any man that walked in. She wasn't exactly a slut, just very friendly with the opposite sex.

Soon, a grey pickup truck pulled up and parked in a space near the door. I wasn't surprised to see Billy hop out of the driver's seat and walk up the steps in his usual brisk, jaunty and easygoing manner. He was wearing a hat and a cable-knit grey sweater with jeans. He looked relaxed and comfortable, and took off his baseball cap when he stepped in the door. He nodded to the receptionist. "G'day," he told her.

Anna grinned at him. "What can I do for you?" she asked, slightly flirtatiously.

"I'm here to see Cindy Washek," he told her. Anna pointed one red-lacquered fingernail in my direction.

"She's right over there, waiting for you," Anna explained.

Billy walked over. "Hey, Cindy," he began, grinning down at me amiably.

"Hey," I replied. "Thanks for inviting me out to lunch."

I got up and followed him toward the door. Anna winked at me as we stepped out the door. Billy led me to his truck and opened the door for me. I hopped in, closed the door, and he climbed into the driver's seat, jamming his cap back on his head. It was a very short ride to the café, and he opened the door for me once more when we had reached our destination. It was nice of him, but he didn't really need to do it, I thought to myself as he held open the door of the Townhouse. There were very few people there, maybe two or three other patrons. Billy selected a cozy, hidden little booth in the back of the room. We went up to the counter and got our drinks, he ordered black coffee and I got hot chocolate. When we got back to our seats, I noticed that he seemed to be looking at me intently. "I'm so glad we were able to get together," he began softly. "I've been thinking of you, Cindy."

I shot him somewhat of a puzzled expression, feeling somewhere between flattered and baffled. "Really?" I asked, taking a sip of my drink. "Why?"

Billy shrugged. "I don't know," he answered, brushing his slanted blond bangs out of his face. "I really enjoyed seeing you the other day."

"It was nice to see you, too," I answered. The conversation at first was stiff and awkward, and I wished it was time to go back to work.

We chatted idly about work and the weather and other somewhat mundane topics, sipping from our drinks. He was nice, but Gad, he was so damn boring! He was genuinely interested in what I said, though, and he smiled at me a lot. I wondered if he was sweet on me or something. Maybe. I asked him about his grad degree and he explained bridge engineering to me, which I actually found pretty interesting. We chatted some more, and I got quite a bit more comfortable with him as our conversation progressed. He must have relaxed too, because he leaned back in his chair. Interestingly enough, he hadn't mentioned Teela. I sort of hoped he wouldn't, but I was out of luck.

"Are you happy with her?" the question came literally out of nowhere, so startling that I even jumped slightly.

I whipped my head around. "Hm?" I asked. He repeated his question, not unkindly, just curious.

I nodded. "Yes, I am," I answered. "Definitely."

He looked at me curiously, analyzing with his engineer's eyes. "So, if you don't mind, how did you two meet, exactly?"

I smiled "Well, actually, it's quite an interesting story. Teela lost her purse in the grocery store, and nearly shot me in the head when I went to return it. When I saw her, I guess I just fell in love."

Billy nodded and chuckled. "So the moral of your story is that sometimes love shoots you in the head?"

I nodded. "Yeah, pretty much," I answered.

He glanced at me, sipping his coffee. "I don't doubt that in the least," he said thoughtfully, cupping his hands around his mug. We were silent for a few moments, sipping our drinks and gazing out the window, until he spoke again. "Have you ever been unsure of your decision to be a lesbian?" he wondered. "I know some people aren't sure."

I shrugged. "Never really thought about it," I answered. "I'm comfortable with it."

"I hate to be rude, but have you ever been with a man?" he asked.

I shook my head, not really wanting to delve into my sex life with him.

"Why?" he continued.

I sighed. "Never been attracted to men," I answered. "It just isn't there. Sexuality is not a decision, Billy, it's innate."

He nodded. "I understand that," he said softly. "I just wonder if you just haven't found the right man yet, you're still young."

I clenched my teeth. "What makes you think I want a man?" I snapped.

He smiled and shrugged. "I didn't mean to offend you," he reassured me. "I just find it rather like saying that you hate broccoli before you even try it. How do you know?"

I was pretty pissed by now. "Look," I growled, my quick-wit temper flaring up. "I didn't come to lunch with you so that you could challenge my sexuality, insult me and Teela, and try to hit on me."

"I was just pointing out that you might not be sure yet," he said softly. "I'm sorry, Cindy."

"That's it," I stood up and threw my napkin on the table. "Goodbye."

I strode toward the door and jerked it open stepping outside. Billy hurried after me.

"Just please let me drive you back," he pleaded.

Pride threatened to get the better of me, but I had no money for a cab and had to get back to work. "Fine," I growled. "But don't touch me or I'll kill you."

Billy grinned as he unlocked the car. "Fair enough," he answered, his eyes twinkling merrily.

Chapter Sixteen

It was a frigid evening in early February, a week or so after the fiasco with Billy Kramer. Things had been sort of tense between Teela and me lately, I had been kind of high strung since my job was on the line, and we were still trying to solve the mystery of McGavin with really not much avail. I had kept an eye on him at work, and Teela was doing some sleuthing at home, but so far we had not been able to unearth anything new. All we knew is he was tracking Teela, but it didn't appear that he was doing it anymore. I had almost searched his office the other day, but then he came back and forgot his wallet, so I was greatly discouraged. I wondered why Teela had been so quiet and uncommunicative lately. I longed to talk to her and find out what was going on, but I was afraid that she might shut me out like she did the other day.

Earlier that day, I was at work, absently filing papers and gazing out the window. McGavin was at a meeting and a lot of people were out, so the hallway was quiet. I sort of enjoyed the mindless, methodical work and had just settled into a rhythm of sorting and stamping and stapling papers when I was interrupted by the sound of someone coming down the hall and coughing slightly. The wall of my desk was in the way, so I couldn't very well see who it was, but as the person neared, I looked up, and it was Billy. He was wearing grey slacks and a sweater, no hat, his hair combed and appeared to be freshly bathed and washed. The subtle scent of lemon and soap filled the air as he approached. I set my pen down and glared up at him, still irritated by his comments the other day. "What are you doing here?" I demanded, maybe a little bit more harshly than I needed to.

Billy's eyes widened and he looked wounded. "Cindy..." he began, "I know I made a mistake, but will you hate me forever?"

I shrugged. "I don't know, maybe," I grumbled, my anger beginning to fade.

He handed me a wrapped package. "This is my way of saying sorry," he told me. "Trust me, I don't want to hit on you, I just want to be friends."

I didn't reply but simply unwrapped the gift. It was a gold-coloured box, small, slender and unmarked. This better not be a ring, I thought, or I might just throw it at his face.

But when I opened the box, it was not a ring. Instead, the box was filled with chocolates that didn't look quite store-bought.

"Did you make these?" I gasped.

Billy nodded and blushed slightly. "Yeah," he answered boyishly. "I learned a thing or two from the kitchen staff at the Townhouse."

I realized how much time it must have taken him to make an entire box of candy just for me. I lifted one of the squares and took a bit, flooded with dark chocolate and creamy, sticky caramel. "Mm, this is delicious," I admitted. "You are quite talented."

He grinned. "Thanks," he answered. "I'll let you get back to work, I just wanted to come and personally tell you that I was wrong and that I'm sorry. I hope you will forgive me," he stuck out his hand.

I shook it tentatively. "Okay, thank you, Billy," I answered. "You're forgiven."

He grinned at me again, gave a little wave and walked off down the hall. "Have a good day," he called over his shoulder, before he disappeared around the corner.
I sighed and took another chocolate. Damn him, I thought. These were really good.

***

So Teela and I were sitting on the couch, watching the news together, but neither one of us was really paying attention. The anchors were blathering on and on with mindless drivel but neither one of us cared. I glanced over at Teela and she seemed closed off to me. I felt kind of a stabbing pain in my chest, stifling a sniffle. I just wanted to get through to her. Finally, the emotion welled up inside me into a tidal wave and I grabbed the remote, shutting the TV off with a crackle of static.

I flung the remote down on the table. "Why are you being so cold?" I asked, my voice threatening to break. Teela turned to face me, her moor-grey eyes wide and misty.

She looked absolutely gorgeous, in a black lace shirt and jeans, crazy socks, her black hair falling all around her face. "What do you mean?" she asked softly, her hands folded in her lap.

I threw my hands up. "Don't give me that load of crap, Teela, you've just been so… cold, lately," I choked out. "I can't feel you, and it hurts."

Teela's eyes flashed like a spark of grey lightning. "You haven't been much better," she shot back. "You've doubted me," she murmured.

I gasped. "Doubting you?" I repeated squeakily, although I knew it was partly true.

She nodded. "Yes," she answered. "I can feel it. Do you trust me, Cindy?"

I nodded. "Of course I do," I answered quietly. "I just can't trust myself always."

Teela stared long and hard at the couch cushion, running her finger over the seam. She said nothing.

"Do you love me, Teela?" I asked her.

She looked up, her eyes full of pain, and shook her head. "How can I love you, Cindy? I've only known you for a few weeks. I think we should glide for a while and figure out what we really want."

Damn, that stung. My eyes filled with tears and my mouth formed a perfect O. "Are you saying you want to end our relationship?" I rasped, nearly speechless.

Thankfully, Teela shook her head. "Not at all," she answered. "I just think we should take some major time to figure out what is good for us. If this is going to work, we need to commit to each other, Cindy, and it is a big step."

I nodded, not quite sure what to say. "Yeah," I agreed. "It is."

We were silent for a moment, until Teela jerked her head up and faced me. "He told you things, didn't he?" she snapped.

I looked up. "Who?" I replied. "McGavin?"

She shook her head. "No. The boy that made the candy. The jerk."

"Billy?" I wondered.

She nodded. "Yeah, him. He told you things about me. He told you our relationship wasn't real."

I was stunned that she knew. "Well..." I began.

She cut me off. "Don't even bother to lie to me," she said quietly. "Because I know the truth."

I was miserable by now. "It isn't my fault that he said that!" I exclaimed.

Teela stroked my hand. "I know," she murmured. "It's just unfortunate."

"Life is unfortunate, Teela," I replied, clasping her hand. I checked the clock and stifled a yawn. "It's almost midnight, I'm tired," I continued. "I have to get up for work tomorrow."

Teela yawned as well. "I'll go to bed, too," she added, and we got up off the couch. In front of my bedroom door I wrapped my arms around her. She barely pecked me on the lips. "Good night, Cindy," she said quietly, and then she walked into her room and closed the door. Sighing, I entered my own room, shut the door behind me and collapsed into bed, pulling the blanket over my head.

Chapter Seventeen

I was driving home from work one night, snow relentlessly blanketing my windshield. I was going about 2mph and my wipers were running at top speed, but even so, it wasn't enough to safely navigate my vehicle through the blizzard. To add insult to injury, McGavin had expected me to work late, so it was well past nine. I was tired and in a bad mood from a long day of work, and my mind was heavily weighted with my home situation as well as the mystery of McGavin. I had had a success in the mystery department today; I had managed to get some information about a secret database that existed on the server. I wasn't sure what the password was or how to even access such a thing, but I figured that I would give the information and server password to Teela so that she could do some investigation. She was sharp as a tack and extremely adept at many things, so I figured that I would ask her to try her hand at hacking the database. Despite the fact that we were working together on this issue, our relationship was filled with tension. We still weren't sure where we were as far as our actual relationship; although there was no way that we could deny the attraction that smoldered between us. We were walking on eggshells and waiting it out, holding back although we both knew that we didn't want to hold back. Damn, it nearly killed me when she left me cold. Maybe she was having trouble dealing with her feelings. I, personally, was pretty open and confident about being with her. Teela, on the other hand, had come from a life of oppression and abuse, and wasn't sure about much of anything. Her way of dealing with things was shutting them out, and it hurt when it was me. I had been talking to Billy a little bit, in no way attracted to him, but just enjoying a friendly face. Other than Billy, Teela, and the people at work, I was completely alone. My parents lived on the other side of the country, they had decided to move back home with the rest of the family, not minding leaving me, their only daughter, behind. They figured I was an adult and could take care of myself.

All of these things were troubling me at the same time as I was trying to get myself home in one piece. I was tempted just to stop and pull over and sleep in my car, but I knew I would freeze to death. *Breathe, Cindy,* I told myself. *Only a few more minutes.* Just then, an avalanche of snow hit my windshield and I was blinded. I went to slam on the brakes, but my car started to slide on the ice. Terrified, I gripped the wheel and just prayed that I wouldn't die. I looked out my driver's side window, and it didn't appear that any traffic was coming, thank God. The car screeched and skidded probably another eight feet before it went off the road with a jarring *thump* and plowed into something soft. I yelled out when the car made impact, even though it wasn't terribly forceful. Shaken and terrified, I looked out the passenger side window to see a pile of white. Shit, I muttered. Right into a snow bank. I sat there for a moment, not sure what to do. I tried and tried to back out but there was no avail. I was stuck. The wheels were spinning and spraying snow all over the place, but the Versa wouldn't budge an inch. There was no way in hell I was getting out and pushing the car in this weather. Sighing, I rested my head on my steering wheel and dug out my phone. I guess I'd have to call someone, even though I didn't want to. Unfortunately, I didn't even know the number for the towing service and it didn't warrant calling 911, so my only options were to call Teela or call Billy. Teela really couldn't do much for me, her car was smaller than mine, and besides, I didn't want to put her in danger by making her come out in this blizzard. Not that she could tow my car anyway. So this left me with a single choice: to call Billy Kramer. With his powerful F-350, he probably could help me out of this mess, and give me a safe lift home. Somehow, I didn't really want to have to call him, but I knew that it wasn't my choice. I dialed his number and lifted my cell phone to my ear, praying that he was home. He picked up on the second ring. "Hello?" he answered.

"Billy, it's Cindy," I told him, skipping the hello.

"Oh, hey, Cindy," he sounded interested. "What's up?"

"My car is stuck in a snow bank somewhere near Main Road and Dale Street," I told him. "Would you be kind enough to come help me? I don't have triple A."

He didn't hesitate to reply. "Absolutely," he answered.

I breathed a sigh of relief. "Oh my God, thank you so much," I sighed gratefully.

"I'll be right there," he told me. "Hang tight."

He said goodbye and hung up. I waited, thinking about whether I should feel bad for using him like this. It was clear that he had a romantic interest in me, and I only wanted to be friends, and tonight I only wanted a tow and lift service. I shook my head. What a damn mess.

Just then, I heard a truck pull up beside me and I rolled down the driver side window, relieved to recognize Billy's F-350, not some creepy man who sought to kidnap me. Billy hopped out of his truck bearing a tow chain, and I got out of my car. I winced when I saw the whole front end imbedded in the snow. "I hope my car will be alright," I told him.

He shrugged. "Oh, I can get this out in a jiffy," he replied, squinting into the swirling snow as he hooked up the tow chain. Once everything was connected correctly, he brushed his gloved hands together, surveyed his work, and opened the passenger door for me. "Hop in," he invited. "We'll get this thing out of here."

I had never been in such a monster truck before, and I wondered if I could even step up there. After a few failed attempts, Billy offered to help me. "Need a boost?" he asked. "I don't want you to fall, those runners are slippery."

My legs cold and weak, I had no choice but to accept. He gripped my hips and boosted me up effortlessly, as if I weighed nothing. I gripped the handle for dear life and climbed into my seat. I noticed just how muscular his arms really were, and figured he must do a lot of heavy-duty outside work. When he hopped into the driver's side and closed the door, I looked at him in disbelief and maybe a slight of admiration. "Wow, you're pretty strong for a math geek," I told him.

He smiled. "Math geeks can surprise you," he replied, his eyes twinkling as he pulled back the gear shift and started to try to pull my Versa out of the snow bank. It took only a few tries before we could feel it come free. "Yup, that's it," he responded.

I started to get out of the car. "I'll drive home," I answered. "If my car still works. Thank you so much."

What was I thinking? Maybe his presence just unnerved me, being in a closed, warm space with such a manly man, especially one who was my friend *and* interested in me. But Billy confirmed how crazy I was. "Don't be silly, Cindy," he waved his hand. "It's below zero out there. You'll freeze. And besides, you'll just end up stuck in another snow bank."

I shrugged with a defeated smile. "You're right," I told him. He simply grinned at me and started the truck with a VROOM.

It didn't take very long for us to arrive at my house, and the ride in his monster truck was a lot smoother than the terrifying, bumpy journey in my car. He parked at the end of the driveway and cut the motor. "Thank you for picking me up," I told him. "I really appreciate it."

He grinned again, softly. "It's no problem," he answered. We sat there in silence for a moment before he cleared his throat nervously. "Um, Cindy?" he asked. "I need to tell you something. It's important."

I turned to face him. "Okay," I answered, not quite sure what he would say, but at the same time I was sure.

He lowered his eyes. "Forgive me," he murmured, and before I knew it he had grasped my chin and lowered his mouth to mine.

I wasn't sure whether to push him away or not, not sure at all, so I stayed there, frozen solid and stiff. He rested his hands on my shoulders and his lips were warm and skilled, and he tasted like mint. The kiss wasn't too bad, actually felt kind of nice, but it was nowhere near what I felt with Teela. I lost myself for a moment, thinking, as he massaged my shoulders with his rough, work-worn hands. I felt stuck in a way, because I was so uncomfortable with his power and suffocated by the maleness that filled the car, but at the same time his hands were heavenly. Damn it, I thought. How did he know my weak spot? I stayed still until he gently moved his hands around to cup my breasts, moaning softly as he squeezed.

Suddenly, I was jolted back to reality and I shoved him off of me, starting to pack up my things. "Billy, I can't," I told him. "You just don't get it!"

He crossed his arms. "You led me on, let me kiss you," he accused. "You could have stopped me!"

"Yes, I should have," I agreed. "Thank you for the lift. Good night." I hopped out of the cab.

"Wait," he hopped out beside me. "How do you plan on getting your car unhooked?"

I was grudgingly silent as he unhooked the chain. I dug through my wallet and slapped a twenty in his hand.
"I'm sorry, Billy." I said sincerely.

Billy stuffed the cash into his pocket, hopped into his cab, and took off with a spray of snow. No doubt he was pissed off that I didn't tip him the way he wanted to be tipped. I fished through my purse and dug out my house keys, letting myself in.

When I got inside, Teela was writing. She looked up, her eyes full of concern. "What happened to you?" she gasped.

"My car got stuck in a snow bank," I explained. "I had to call Billy to pull me out. He has an F-350."

Teela nodded, her eyes narrowing at the mention of his name. "Well, I'm glad you weren't hurt," she replied.

Is that all she had to say? I wanted to tell her how tired I was of her coldness, but I didn't have the energy to start an argument tonight.

"Good news," I told her briskly. "I've learned of a secret database of McGavin's. How are you at database hacking?"

Teela put a finger to her temple and thought. "Well, I could give it a try," she answered. "I've done hacking before."

I explained how I found out about the database and gave her the password. "I will get to work on this tomorrow," she told me with a nod. She glanced at the clock. "It's late, Cindy, I had better get to bed."

I watched her rise from the couch and start putting away her writing stuff. She headed into the other room, but I called after her. "Teela, wait!" I called, maybe a little more urgently than I needed to.

She whipped around. "Yes?" she asked, seeing my pained expression.

All I wanted was to throw my arms around her but I refrained, afraid she would push me away. "I just wanted to say good night," I said softly.

She looked at me for a moment, her eyes flickering; no doubt she was fighting a mental war with herself. I stepped toward her and pulled her into a hug. She stood stiffly for a moment, before her body relaxed and she slipped her arms around me as well. We stayed like that for a few moments, and she finally drew back and gently touched her lips to mine. "Good night, Cynthia," she whispered. I wanted to hold on to her forever, but eventually she gently pulled away and headed into her bedroom. I touched my lips with the tip of my finger, amazed at how one kiss with her got my heart racing. It was a good start, I thought, and I hoped that we would be able to make up.

Chapter Eighteen

My mood the next day wasn't too bad, I was glad that Teela and I had started to make up, and I had hoped for more progress. Work wasn't too tedious, because McGavin, strangely enough, wasn't there. That was very odd because I couldn't remember the last time McGavin had missed work, he was there every day, rain or shine.
I wondered what Teela was doing, what she was thinking of. I pictured her with her pen poised over her notebook, a pensive faraway look on her pretty face. She had been wearing the most beautiful jade-green silk top this morning, and she looked breathtaking. I was working on some files when I heard my cell phone ring. That's unusual, I thought, because my cell phone almost never rang. After the fiasco with Billy the night before, I hoped to God that it wasn't him. Ugh, I shuddered. Never again. That was exactly why I wasn't interested in men. They were so forceful, and always wanted to push things as far as they possibly could with a woman as quickly as they possibly could. They just wanted sex and nothing else. God help the bastards, I grumbled, shaking my head. I abruptly stopped typing, and fished my phone out of my purse. I checked the display, thankful it wasn't Billy. Teela? I hoped nothing was wrong, because she usually called

me on my desk line to save me minutes on my phone. This must be important, I thought.

I flipped open my scratched track phone. "Teela?" I asked in wonder. "What's up?"

"Cindy, I have astounding news," she whispered, her voice really low. "I had to call you on the cell phone so no one overhears."

"Go on," I prompted eagerly. "What is it?"

"Well," Teela continued. "I hacked the database."

I put my hand over my mouth. "My God, you're brilliant," I said quietly, careful not to talk too loud. "What did you find?"

The answer that came damn near blew my socks off. "Turns out, McGavin and Frank are mixed up in a racket and illegally trading some kind of radioactive surveillance software."

I gasped. "What?" I asked. "Are you serious?"

"Completely," Teela replied gravely. "All of the trade routes and records were stored in a folder on this database. Frank has access to this illegal software, and instead of money, sometimes he would ask for information about me."

I snapped my fingers. "That explains it," I answered. "How he found you at my house."

"It explains all of it," Teela added. She lowered her voice some more. "There's bad news, too."

"How bad?" I asked fearfully.

"Horrendous," Teela replied. "They plan to stage some kind of takeover with this software that will allow them to infiltrate people's homes, leaving no evidence at all."

My eyes widened. "Oh no," I gasped. "We have to stop them!"

"We will," Teela assured me. "I am planning to print out these pages right now and turn them in to the police department."

"Perfect..." I started to say, but then I heard a scream and a crash on the other end of the line.

"Teela!" I shouted. "Are you okay?" but the phone went dead. Immediately, I leapt into action, grabbed my coat and sprang up from my desk. I stuffed my cell phone into my pocket and raced out the door, past Maria, the receptionist. "Gotta go!" I yelled as I busted the front door of the firm open. Maria looked alarmed, but she must have figured that I was in serious trouble. Outside, the snow was swirling, but I fought through the storm of light flurries and hopped into my Versa, throwing it into reverse and tearing out of the parking lot with a screech of tires. I drove as fast as I could, narrowly avoiding getting into an accident. When I pulled up to my house, my fears were confirmed: something was happening. The front door was ajar and there was a beat-up dirty black van parked in front of the house. I saw two masked men hauling Teela out of the house and toward the van. She was screaming and struggling, but it was in vain. One of the men made a quick motion with his hands, and I didn't see exactly what happened, but Teela's struggling grew weaker until she collapsed, limp in their arms. They tossed her in the back of the van and roared off. I clapped my hand over my mouth and stifled a gasp or scream. "No!" I shouted, tears running down my face. "Oh no!"

Breathe, I told myself, and I fished my cell phone out of my purse to call the police. I had just pressed "TALK" when the battery died. I pressed again, but there was no avail. I had no idea what was going on, but I didn't have time to waste. I threw the car into gear and peeled out of my driveway, following the erratic tracks that led off down the road. I drove much faster than I probably should have, but it was an emergency. I followed the tracks until they stopped, and then I was stumped. The road forked in two ways, and it was hard to see. The only advantage was that the van was huge and hard to maneuver, so it was slowed down. I looked to both sides and saw a black shape rounding the corner. I hit the accelerator and went after them, not noticing the other black van that was careening along behind me. Suddenly, in

my rearview mirror I could see the driver of the behemoth
behind me stick some sort of object out the window. BAM!
The sound of a gun firing caused me to swerve and nearly
lose control. I ducked as a bullet splintered my windshield. I
didn't know how much further I could go on like this. There
was another staccato burst of gunfire and to my horror, the
car stopped and started to slide. I slammed on the brake and
screamed as it rammed into a snowdrift. Those bastards had
shot out my tires! I knew that I would be next. What was I
thinking, trying to go after these guys myself? I sat there for a
moment, shaken, until I saw the van slowing to a halt and two
men with guns coming toward my car. Terrified for my life, I
flung the door open and started running, hoping that the
snowstorm would camouflage me. There were no houses in
sight. We must be in the country, I observed, but I had no
idea where I was. I had been tailing the van for nearly an hour
and had never been in this part of town. Maybe there was a
way I could catch up, I thought, and I could see a lone
building in the distance through the fog. There I would go, I
decided, and I would get help. I took off running, feeling the
adrenaline surging through my veins. My legs burned and my
lungs burned as I sprinted across the field, glad I was in such
good shape. I could hear the men thundering behind me, and
one of them shouted, "After her!"

There were a few trees lining the open space, and I
darted between them. I ran until I felt like I could run no
more, and crouched behind a snowdrift. I peered over the top
tentatively, and thankfully, the men were nowhere to be seen.
The building in the distance was closer now, and if I walked
another half a mile I could probably get to it. I stood up on
numb and shaky legs, glancing behind me, before I continued
on. Keep going, Cindy," I spurred myself on. "You can do it."
I was going to do this, going to do it for Teela. I realized how
much I loved her and how I would even give my life for her. I
trekked across the barren field, through about probably a foot
of deep snow. To ease my way, I counted backwards from

100. "One hundred… Ninety nine… Ninety eight," I chanted under my breath as I strode along. "Ninety seven… Ninety six… Ninety five…. Ninety four…"

Ninety four, I thought to myself, Plutonium's atomic number. Radioactive. Then is where things went wrong. The word ninety-four was barely off of my lips when I heard a shout and felt a sharp pain in the back of my head. The landscape spun around, and I remember the sensation of falling forward. I don't know what I fell on, because everything went completely black.

Chapter Nineteen

I awoke, dazed, disoriented, and cold, with my face pressed into some sort of splintery, hard, dark wood floor. I was cold to the point of feeling like my entire body was numb, not to mention extremely sore. *Where the hell am I*, I thought, wondering how I got into some dark, dingy place with a splintery musty-smelling wood floor pressed into my face. I rubbed my eyes and slowly it all came back to me, the kidnapping of Teela, and how I had valiantly tried to save her then I blacked out. I still didn't really know where I was or if there was anyone in the room with me. As I was laying there trying to analyze my surroundings I was momentarily unable to get up, so I just hung out for a moment, thinking. Suddenly, I was jarred from my thoughts and semiconscious state by the sound of a soft moan somewhere near me. Every nerve ending in my system crackled to life and I would have whipped my head around if I could have. Teela! Teela was here! I knew that sound, I knew it very well. I mustered up all of my energy and cleared my throat.

"Teela?" I rasped.

She stirred for a moment. Finally, she answered, "Cindy?"

We were both just so glad to be together, although we were both lying prone on the floor. With great effort, I managed to sit up, trying to ignore the lump on my head. One of those bastards had chucked a rock at me, I remembered now. I looked down at Teela, and she looked pale and thin, her ankles bound, constricting her circulation. I moved to help her up, but then I heard a tremendous crash and creak as the door thundered open and a masked man came in with a tin tray with two slices of bread, a slab of cheese, and two tin cups of water. "Here," he thrust the food at us. "The boss told me to bring this to you."

"Who's the boss?" I asked daringly.

The man looked irritated. "You'll find out, all right," he warned, and with that, the masked behemoth of a man exited with a dramatic slam of the door, followed by the sound of a deadbolt clicking into place.

As soon as the man had left, I flipped open my dull pocketknife that was disguised as part of my belt. I sawed at Teela's bonds until they loosened, and I gently helped her to a sitting position. Her face was wan and pale, and I dipped my fingers in my water glass and wiped her face with my sleeve. I handed her one of the cups, which she drank from gratefully, weakly. I stroked her cheek and threaded my fingers through her long black hair. "Oh, Teela," I whispered. "If we have to be imprisoned, at least we are together."

She nodded and draped her arm around my shoulders. "Oh, Cynthia," she murmured, "I'm sorry I was so cold to you."

"Nonsense," I whispered against her lips, kissing her gently before I pulled away. "Let's eat," I told her. "We're gonna need our strength for escape."

We ate in silence, and we were both feeling better by the time we had finished with our meager rations. Once renewed, we thought about how to escape. There was no light in the room except for a dull filtering of light through dirty wooden slats on what used to be a window. "I wonder how high up we are," I mused to Teela, who was leaning against the wall.

"My guess is that we're at least second story," she answered. "That type of slatted window is not usually first-floor."

"Well, I'll take a look," I offered, and I quietly rose to my feet. I grimaced when the floor creaked loudly, and tiptoed over to the window. I started trying to peel away at the slats but they were too strong and I was getting splinters. "Ow, damn it!" I muttered as a sharp edge grazed my hand. I continued to fiddle around with it, until I had made a big enough crack to barely see outside. What I saw was that we were about two stories off the ground, and there was what looked like a farmhouse and silo, both of which were rotting and falling down. "I think I know what our prison is!" I told Teela excitedly in a hushed whisper. "We're in an abandoned barn or farmhouse!"

"I have good news, too," Teela whispered, holding up an object. I squinted to see it in the dark. "I found a broken pitchfork handle over here under this dusty straw."

"That's wonderful," I whispered back. "Keep it out of sight. I might have an escape plan."

Teela and I celebrated our small success very quietly, and quickly kissed each other on the lips. Despite the fact that we were trapped in a rotting abandoned farmhouse in the dark, Teela Grant was still hot as hell and her kiss turned my blood to molten honey flushing through my veins. I plowed my fingers through her hair and she flicked her tongue in and out of my mouth with an artistic friction. When we pulled apart, I elbowed her playfully. "We'll never escape if you incapacitate me like that, Miss Grant," I teased her in a murmur.

She elbowed me right back, then trailed her fingertips down my arm. "Oh yeah?" she murmured. "Well, we might escape here but you won't escape me, Cynthia."

I shivered with pleasure and smiled sultrily at her, even though it was dark. "I can't wait," I breathed.

We sat there holding hands and propped up against the wall, and eventually we fell asleep in each other's arms.

Suddenly, sometime later, not sure what time it was, Teela and I were both jarred awake by the door thundering open once again. I awoke with a start and jumped, grabbing onto Teela for dear life, and she did the same. A man with a mask and evil eyes stood there, grinning down at us. "Well, if it ain't the most beautiful faggots I've ever seen," he drawled. Teela stiffened and froze with terror, her mouth hanging open. "I'm the big boss of this operation. How genius of you two to come find me."

I knew that voice, and Teela must have too, because it wasn't McGavin's. The two of us sat there, not saying a word. The man rubbed his hands together and peeled his mask back just enough that we could see his face. Teela blanched and stifled a gasp or scream, and my mouth fell open with shock and horror. Frank!

"I thought you were in jail or dead," I gasped.

Frank laughed. "A feeble hope, maybe, but no, I'm alive and well," he rubbed his hands together. "If you want proof of my vitality, I'd be happy to oblige," he leered at Teela, who looked petrified.

"That won't be necessary," I bit off.

"Perhaps it won't be," he replied rather quickly, shrugging his shoulders. "Because what I came up here to tell you two is that you two are a danger to my business, and I'm afraid we can't have that," he mock pouted, letting the severity of his words sink in.

When we still didn't reply, he continued. "Not very talkative, eh?" he taunted. "Well, that's alright, gals, because I'm gonna give you two choices."

"Hey, Mr. Potato Head," I snapped, losing patience. "Skip the riffraff, just get on with it."

He didn't retaliate to my tone. Instead, he continued in a smooth, oily voice. "Want to play that way?" he asked sweetly, his voice dripping with sarcasm. "Here's the deal.

Originally, the guys thought I should just kill you both, but I disagreed. Not because I have any hang-ups about killing you, but that you could be of use to me."

Teela was silent; her misty eyes fixed far away, absolutely unmoving, looking like a statue. Her stance unnerved him slightly because he glanced over quickly before continuing. "Choice number one," he purred. "I can kill you both as planned. Quick and simple death." He drew his pistol. "I have a very correct shot, and you can kiss each other goodbye and decide who dies first."

"…and choice two?" I prompted, trying to figure out how to escape.

"And choice two," he ticked off a two on his fingers. "You both are allowed to live unharmed, but you have to stay here and serve me…"

He broke off and moved toward us, bending to finger a strand of Teela's hair. "You, my dear, would be the servant of my bed. You would have full access to fine meals, and I'd buy you fine clothes, but you would have to pleasure me at my convenience, any time, all the time."

Teela didn't reply, but slapped his hand away.

"And you," he turned to me, still looming over us. "Would be the servant of my house, pick up all of my trash, do anything I asked you to. Cook, clean, and help with my business. You would sleep in the loft up here, alone. And as far as both of you, if you disobey me I will beat you or kill you. What is your choice?"

"Will you give us some time to decide, sir?" I asked in my most velveteen voice.

"I guess," he grunted gruffly. "But those are the only choices. You have until sundown, or I will assume that you are choosing option number one."

With that, he whirled on his heel and slammed the heavy door, locking it behind him.

"My god, what a monster," I fumed. "If he touches you, Teela, I swear to God I will castrate him."

Teela nodded, shakily. She seemed to be in some state of pseudo- semi-unconsciousness. "We need to get out of here, Cindy," she whispered. The direness of the situation suddenly dawned on me, that we were trapped in an old rotting barn with a couple hours to make a critical choice: either meet our death or be enslaved. Never in my life had I ever been in such a position or dreamed that I'd be in such a position.

Teela suddenly erupted into a whispered stream of vulgar expletives. She turned to me. "I swear to God, Cindy, I'd slit my wrists and shoot myself in the head before I'd let that vile, lowdown, motherfucking cocksucker son of a douchebag touch me," she slammed her fist down on the floor with an emphatic bang. It was clear how traumatized she had been in her life, and I was suddenly flooded with new energy. "Let's get planning," I muttered. "Where's the pitchfork?"

"Over here," Teela mouthed.

I rose quietly, and helped Teela to her feet, even though she was weak. I hoped she would be able to make it to the escape. I tiptoed over to the window and winced when the floor creaked. "Shit," I muttered, hoping that the guys wouldn't hear the noise and come up to tie us up again. Teela handed me the broken handle that had been stashed in the corner, and I began an attempt to pry the slats away. It was a lot easier said than done, the old wood was a lot tougher than it looked. I chipped away at the first board and was immediately slapped in the face by a gust of icy wind. Wincing, I stepped back.

"Cindy, if we do it this way we'll never get out," Teela pointed out.

"True," I answered, and the two of us chipped away at a little faster. It took quite a while, but eventually we made a hole big enough that we could look out. I peered through the moderate gap, and thankfully, there was a thin-barred rusty metal ladder attached to the side of the building. I gasped in dismay. There was no way in hell that the two of us could manage to climb out the window and safely make it down that ladder, which was most likely lethally slippery and covered with ice. Teela came over to take a look and her face went ashen. "I'm afraid of heights, Cindy," she whispered.

"I'll go first," I offered. "But right now we need to finish chipping away these window slats."

"Just swing hard and smash it," Teela suggested. "It can't hurt."

I looked out and it was beginning to get dark around the edges of the sky. It was clear that we would have to take a risk, because Frank would be coming back up at nightfall. Besides, if it got dark, we could never make our way down the ladder.

"Here goes," I muttered, and pulled back, swinging the metal bar with all of my might. It gashed quite a hole in the wood, sending sheaves of splintered slats to their fall. Good start, but still not big enough. Bracing myself, I swung it again, this time making a wider gap.

"One more good swing should do it," Teela observed. I closed my eyes, braced myself and put every ounce of strength into the last blow. There was a tremendous splintering crash as the entire window frame tilted and fell away, leaving a perfectly sized gaping hole right at the top of the ladder. The rotted wood, dust, dirt and sediment sailed down to the ground, the landing luckily muffled by the deep snow. Now that we had smashed through the window, the next order of business was the arduous, slippery descent down the ice-covered ladder. As terrifying as it was, I had entered survival mode and was just determined to escape the terrible fate that awaited Teela and me if we stayed.

"Don't panic," I told Teela. "It will be okay. I will go first, it really isn't that far."

Teela nodded shakily. "I can't look," she told me, and covered her eyes as I turned and lowered my foot onto the top rung. It was slippery, but not as slippery as I had feared, and luckily the step was sound. I stepped down again, praying as I gripped the superior rung with a death grip, and I feared that I might break the metal. Step by torturous step, I backed down the ladder, only losing my grip once. I steeled my mind as I numbly stepped down, until I finally reached the last rung and hopped the three feet to the ground. "Come on down," I told Teela. She seemed to gather herself, more confident since I had made it, and gingerly stepped down as I had. She faltered a bit at first but spurred herself on, step over step as I had done. I could hear her chanting a prayer as she stepped down, and finally she touched down beside me. I threw my arms around her and we kissed passionately, so glad that we had made the climb. Our relief was short-lived, though, because there was a tremendous splintering noise as the metal ladder detached from the wall and tipped precariously toward us. Shrieking, we ducked out of the way just in time as it crashed into the dirty snow beside us.

We were about to start running when there was a shout and the door to the adjacent building busted open. "They're escaping!" someone yelled. That was it. Teela and I immediately sprang into action and started running, somehow fighting through the deep snow, our survival instincts making our speed almost superhuman. We had a fair head start when we heard Frank shouting something behind us. There was quite a blizzard, snow flurries stinging my already frozen and numb face, and I could see nothing ahead of me, could barely see Teela who was a few feet ahead of me. I figured that this snowstorm might work to our advantage if the men couldn't see us, so we kept going. Just then, the sound of a gunshot pierced the air. We ducked, and the bullet whistled overhead. I don't even know how long we ran when we heard police sirens coming down the road. How the police had found us must have been a miracle of God, because three or four squad cars pulled up along with an ambulance. The men began running, but the officer announced over the bullhorn that they were under arrest. Most of the men dropped their weapons, but Frank fired one more shot into the trees, splintering a piece of rotting timber that was directly over Teela, who was a few paces ahead of me. I screamed as the heavy log crashed down, and Teela managed to avoid the brunt of the blow, but the end nicked her in the head, and I screamed out as she crumpled to the ground and lay there motionless. The EMT's immediately leapt out and fought through the thick snow, loading her onto a gurney. An assortment of police officers handcuffed the criminals and read them their rights, while one of the female officers offered me a blanket and invited me into the warm police car. I was sobbing uncontrollably, and the officer gently offered me a tissue. She told me her name was Officer Bricker but I could call her Susan.

"I think your friend will be okay," she reassured me. "They are taking her to the hospital now."

"How did you find us?" I asked her shakily. "It's a miracle."

Susan nodded gravely. "Yes, in a way it was. Actually a combination of things. A few of your neighbors saw your friend get kidnapped and heard the entire ruckus. We had had a report of trespassers on this abandoned farm, so we decided to investigate. A top-of-the-line FBI investigator assisted us, and we were able to find you two in a short time."

"Thank God," I breathed. "Take me to the hospital, please. I want to be with my girlfriend."

"If I may ask, what's her name?" Susan inquired.

"Teela," I replied, my voice full of love.

Susan offered me a look filled with sympathy. "What a lovely name," she sighed. "In fact, I have a girlfriend too. It took a long time for my family to accept our relationship, but it was worth it. I can see how much you love your Teela, and it is my advice that you never ever lose her."

"Thanks," I told Susan. "It means a lot."

She smiled. "No problem," she answered, and I closed my eyes, curling up in the back of the police car with the blanket, exhausted.

Sara J. Kuhrman

Chapter Twenty

It was nearly nightfall when Officer Susan and I arrived at the hospital. I hated hospitals, and winced as soon as I opened the door, the sickly sterile antiseptic smell overpowering me as I stepped into the industrially furnished room. I walked over to the desk where a thin-faced redheaded college-aged clerk sat typing at a computer, enclosed in a dingy grey office. When she swiveled her chair to face me I saw that her name was Debby.

"Yes?" she asked; her voice nasal and muted.

"Hi. I'm Cynthia Washek. I'm looking for my girlfriend, Miss Teela Grant," I told her, showing my driver's license.

Debby shook her head. "I'm sorry," she told me, with no pity whatsoever. "But I cannot disclose patient information."

I shot Susan a helpless look, and she got the hint. Susan stepped up to the desk. "I'm Officer Susan Bricker," she introduced herself, showing her badge. "These two ladies have just been rescued from an emergency situation. As an officer of the law, I ask that you will let Cindy see her girlfriend."

Debby sighed. "Very well," she answered primly, scanning her records. "Approximately ten minutes ago, the EMT's wheeled a dark-haired girl in here on a gurney, but I didn't see where they took her. Listed as Teela C. Grant. Ask

107

Molly, one of the ER nurses, she would know," Debby pointed an unmanicured fingernail to a blonde nurse in the corner.

I walked over to the blonde nurse who was dumping a trash bin. "Are you Molly?" I asked her.

She looked up with a pleasant smile, though slightly startled. "Yes, I am," she answered.

"I'm Cindy," I told her. "And Debby at the desk told me that you might know where my girlfriend, Teela Grant, is. Apparently she came in on a stretcher about ten minutes ago,"

Molly thought for a moment. "Dark hair?" she asked. I nodded.

Molly smiled sadly. "Well, about ten minutes ago they wheeled in a real pretty gal with dark curly hair. Poor thing looked frozen to the bone, out cold. They're working on her as we speak."

"Oh, no, Teela…" I breathed, and then I turned to Molly, my eyes wide. "What's wrong with her, is she okay?"

Molly shrugged. "Well, I'm not exactly sure, but I know our best doctor, Megan Paloura, is working on her right now. I understand that she has a bad concussion and is in a coma."

My hand flew to my mouth and tears stung my eyes, and before I could stop them, began streaming down my face. Molly tried to comfort me, but I heard nothing, my tears spiraling out of control. She ferried back and forth, giving updates and going from room to room.

The hours became a blur to me and I sank down on the bench, sobbing uncontrollably. Officer Susan Bricker was nice enough to stay with me and she awkwardly put her arm around me and tried to comfort me.

Finally, a woman in a white coat emerged and strode toward me. She stood about six foot two and had bright copper-red hair, a small face, and freckles across the bridge of her nose. She extended her hand. "I'm Dr. Megan Paloura," she told me. "You're Teela's girlfriend, right?"

I nodded and sniffled. I looked up, pinning her with a hopeful stare. "Teela isn't dead, is she?" I whispered.

The entire weight of the universe settled on the time between when the sentence left my lips and when the doctor answered. She drew in a breath. "No, she isn't. when we brought her in, her heartbeat was weak and her body temp was dangerously low, but we fixed her up. She does have a concussion and was hit pretty hard on the back of the head. Luckily, we were able to treat her just in time."

"Will there be any permanent brain damage from the concussion?" I asked.

Dr. Paloura shook her head. "I highly doubt it, although it is still a remote possibility. She was treated very promptly, which is a good sign. She should be waking up anytime now, and that is when we will tell if any permanent damage was done. But, I assure you that the signs are good that she will walk away fine."

"Thank God," I breathed.

After the doctor went back into the other room, I succumbed to exhaustion and fell asleep hunched over on the hard, cold hospital bench, leaning against Officer Bricker's motherly shoulder.

Sometime a few hours later, I was gently shaken awake. "Cindy?" Susan asked gently. "The doctor has news for you."

I looked up expectantly, but Dr. Paloura's face yielded not one way or the other. "Please tell me," I begged.

"Good news," the doctor answered briskly. "Miss Grant has woken from her coma. We will be performing some tests and scans to see if she has sustained any or brain damage, but things look very promising as of right now. She is just resting right now, and very sleepy from the medications, but you may see her if you like."

"Oh, I will," I answered, rising to my feet. "I'm going to use the restroom first, though."

"Go right ahead," Doctor Paloura answered. "Ms. Grant is in room 32B. Just be prepared, she looks a lot worse than she is."

"Okay," I answered gravely. I stopped in the restroom real quickly to dab my eyes. The girl that looked back at me from the mirror was an abomination: grey tear-stained skin, heavy bags under the eyes, unwashed brown hair pulled back into a ponytail. I splashed water on my face and swigged from my travel-size mouthwash to rid my mouth of the gross morning taste. Then, I headed down the hall to room 32B and paused with my hand on the doorknob.

I took a deep breath, said a quick prayer, and knocked lightly on the door. A nurse opened it and, seeing that it was me, she let me in. "She's sleeping right now," the nurse told me. "But so far she's doing great."

I could have hugged the nurse. She stepped aside and I cautiously entered the room, remembering Dr. Paloura's words about Teela looking worse than she was.

My heart threatened to come up my throat and my hand flew to my mouth when I saw Teela laying there in the bed, thin and pale, in a hospital gown with a light blanket covering her. Her eyes were closed and her arm outstretched, her dark hair spilling onto the pillow around her face. She was hooked up to all kinds of monitors and an IV tube, but her breathing seemed to be deep and rhythmic. At least she was sleeping peacefully. I hated to wake her, so I just gently sat down next to her on the bed and lovingly stroked her pale pretty face and thick dark hair. "Oh, Teela," I murmured. "I love you."

Eventually, she must have become aware of my presence because she stirred and opened her eyes. Her gray eyes were misty and groggy but clearly lit with recognition. "Cynthia?" she whispered weakly, her voice ever so slight. I took her hand, the one that wasn't wrapped in a bandage with the IV tube. She squeezed my hand and smiled at me, and I continued to gently stroke her hair. Dr. Paloura bustled in and out, and told me that it was normal if she drifted off to sleep intermittently, which she did. We didn't talk much; I just sat there holding her hand until she would gently drift off, her hand still clasped in mine. I also drifted in and out of sleep myself, and although her voice was soft and garbled, I could have sworn that Teela told me she loved me. I fell asleep at her side in that folding chair, and one of the nurses must have scooted me over, but there was no way I was going to leave my Teela's side.

Chapter Twenty-One

For the next few days, I stayed in the hospital with Teela. She was recovering nicely, and I was eternally thankful when Dr. Paloura told me that there was no permanent brain damage from Teela's concussion. She was still weak and groggy from the pain medications and had some minor lacerations from our ordeal at the abandoned farmhouse. The very next day after she had been admitted, they moved her from the acute care unit to a private room where they had machines monitoring her heart rate and other functions. She was still hooked up to the IV to keep her fluid levels steady. All of that time, I sat by her bedside in the dingy hospital room as the TV droned on and on. Teela was listless and restless, and I could tell that she just wanted some quiet. Finally, I rose and shut the thing off, sick of the mindless drivel that it blared. She sank back and closed her eyes, relieved.

It was about two o'clock in the morning, after a nurse had finished doing Teela's hourly blood test, and I was sleeping in the frayed chair in the corner when I awoke to the sound of soft sniffling. I shot up in my chair and rubbed my eyes. "Teela, what's wrong?" I whispered, alarmed. "Should I call the nurse?"

"No," Teela whispered, and then she broke into tears again. "It's just that this is all… *his* fault."

I sat down next to her on the bed and took her hand. "Shh, Teela, It's okay," I murmured. "Forget about him. He is gone."

She nodded weakly. "I have nightmares," she whispered. "I hate him, Cindy! I hate him!"

"You're strong, Teela, you made it," I whispered, stroking her hair. "It's all done. In fact, Frank is dead."

Teela looked up in shock. "Oh my God," she murmured.

"Sheriff called me a short time ago and told me that Frank shot himself before they could disarm him and that the county coroner has just pronounced him dead." I told her.

"I shouldn't be relieved, but I am" Teela answered quietly. "That would make me a terrible person."

"No, it wouldn't," I reassured her. "You have every right. It's just the way things were meant to be. Don't blame yourself. He was a sick, psychotic bastard who did terrible things to people. Don't think about the past anymore, Teela, just think about the present and future."

I pulled out my mp3 player, which was unique in the fact that it came with tiny speakers. I set it up on the bedside table and put on one of our favorite songs, a flowing, soft, and new-age ballad with a quiet thrumming beat, sung in Spanish by a Venezuelan woman. I had taken Spanish in high school, so I knew quite a bit of it, and I knew the song by heart.

"Cynthia?" Teela asked softly. "Will you please sing to me?"

"Certainly," I whispered, and I began to sing softly along with the song, all the while holding her hand. I skimmed my thumb gently along the side of her hand as I crooned to her, and I felt her relax. Luckily, the hospital was quiet at the moment, very little going on. Teela sighed softly and lightly, weakly squeezed my hand, her thin fingers flicking over the inside of my wrist. Soon after the song had finished, her hand went limp in mine and she fell asleep. I followed soon behind.

Chapter Twenty-Two

Finally, that glorious day rolled around when Teela could be released from the hospital. Dr. Paloura gave us a packet of information on concussions and told us that everything would be okay. We said good-bye to all of the hospital staff who had treated her, and since she was still a bit weak from her hospital stay, I wheeled her down in a wheelchair. I pushed her across the linoleum floor of the lobby, and through the revolving glass door. The late-afternoon February sun was shining through the clouds, but it was still frigid outside, the icy air greeting us with its polar kiss. Teela shivered and pulled her blanket tighter around her body. "Seems I've forgotten what winter feels like," she commented.

"Tell me about it," I agreed. "It's kind of refreshing after that stuffy hospital room."

"Definitely," she replied quietly. We didn't talk much as I wheeled her to the car, we didn't have much to say, both immensely worn out from our arduous ordeal. I was just so thankful that she was okay, and I said a silent prayer of thanks, smiling up into the golden afternoon sun.

When we got back to my house and I swung open the front door, it felt cold and desolate, as if we had been gone for a year rather than a few days. Well, it certainly felt like a year, I thought to myself. Whew, it had been terrible the last few days. The kidnapping, the hospital, etc. "Damn," I muttered to Teela. "We've been through hell and back."

She nodded. "That's for sure," she agreed, though she was very subdued. I understood, after being through that whole experience. Her black hair was flat and she had dark circles under her eyes, she looked weak and pale and thin.

"We haven't had anything to eat since this morning," I commented. "Would you like me to cook something?"

Teela shook her head. "Not now," she answered. "I want to get cleaned up first. I feel awful."

I was quite aware of the grubby, haven't-showered-for-three-days, germy sickly hospital feeling, and it clung to me like a wet moldy blanket. "Yeah, good idea," I told her. "I'm sure you will feel better. I will help you if you need it; I don't want you to fall."

Teela fixed me with her misty gray eyes. "Please do, I am a bit unsteady on my feet," she requested softly, our forgotten phantom passion lurking beneath the surface of her voice. Even as bedraggled and disheveled as she looked, Teela knew how to work it. The quiet plea in her voice sent a shiver dancing over my skin, but I was a bit nervous. Technically, she was still recovering, and we hadn't gotten close with each other for quite some time. Did she still want to be with me? I didn't know. I decided to just let things go as they would and let her initiate if she was going to, because she was the one with the delicate health. I pulled my hair back into a utility ponytail and rolled up my sleeves and started washing out the bathtub.

Teela stepped into the bathroom behind me, wrapped in a grey towel. "Nervous about something, Cindy?" she asked me.

I shook my head. "Nah," I answered. "I've just never… um, given anyone a bath before."

Teela smiled. "You don't make much of a nursemaid, then," she joked.

"Well, I never said I wouldn't give it a try," I countered softly, offering her my hand.

"Great, so I'm just your guinea pig?" she teased, taking my hand.

I shook my head. "Guinea pig doesn't describe at all," I replied. "I was thinking more along the lines of…"

My train of thought was broken when Teela dropped her towel. "God, Teela, you're beautiful," I blurted before I could think. She smiled and her eyes softened as she stepped into the shower, but she shook her head.

"Thanks, Cindy, but I've got a lot of scars," she answered quietly.

It was true that she had some scars and faded bruises, but she in her natural state was a work of art. Her skin was pale, almost glass-like, smooth and satiny from head to toe. She was small and thin, and the spidery network of veins danced mystically beneath her skin.

"Your scars make you strong," I murmured to her, trailing my lathered hands lightly down her arms. "You're beautiful."

She blushed but took my hand. "Hop in. You'll be able to help me better," she said abruptly.

I was thankful to peel my grubby, grungy clothes off and I stepped into the spray alongside of her.

She scrubbed off with her washcloth while holding fast to the shower bar, and soon she was ready to wash her hair. "Want help?" I asked her, and she nodded. I pumped some shampoo into my palm and softly told her to turn around. She did, and leaned back with her eyes closed, the inky cascade of her hair falling halfway down her back. "Your hair is so lovely, Teela," I told her, sliding a silky strand of her hair through my fingers as I worked in the shampoo.

"Thanks," she murmured with a sigh, her eyes still closed, relaxing under my touch. I helped her rinse her hair clean and lathered on the conditioner but I couldn't help but run my hands through her slick wet hair once again, captivated. She was like some sort of sea enchantress with a hold on me, shaking my head, I realized that I hadn't even picked up my washcloth yet and was trying to wash myself with a phantom washcloth. Teela caught on to the reason for my clumsiness and with a twinkle in her eye she handed me the correct square of fabric. "I believe you're looking for this?" she teased, a flicker of amusement on her lips, but I could tell she was flattered because her cheeks flushed slightly red.

I took it with a laugh. "Yes, I am, in fact," I countered. "Where did you ever find this?"

I scrubbed down fairly quickly with my washcloth then tilted my head back to wash my hair. "I'll help you," Teela offered softly from behind me, lathering up her hands with shampoo.

"Are you sure?" I asked. "Don't fall."

"Close your eyes, Cynthia," she told me, answering my question. I willingly did as she asked and tilted my head back. She lathered up her hands and laced her thin fingers through my hair, gently and thoroughly massaging my scalp. She deeply and adeptly washed my hair with the grace of a hairdresser and it felt wonderful.

"Man, that feels nice," I told her. "I don't think I've ever had my hair washed this well."

"Yes?" Teela asked me softly. I kept my eyes closed as she massaged my scalp and gently tilted me back to rinse.

"I never want you to stop," I breathed. Slowly, sensuously, she slid her hands down and rested them ever so lightly on my shoulders. The touch of her hands was mystical and sprite-like, as if she were barely touching me at all. She kept her hands rested there for a few moments before she started to gently but deeply knead my shoulders and upper back. One thing about Teela Grant was that she knew how to give a mean massage. I damn near lost myself with her hands on me, and silver pinpricks of stardust flashed behind my closed eyelids when her golden hands became restless and wayward. I turned around and slid my hands down her sides, slick and smooth with hot, soapy water. I stepped into her arms and took her chin, leaning in for a kiss. She twined her arms around my neck and we locked lips as our hot, slippery skin was immediately touching, immediately obliterating all levels of consciousness except her, her hands, her lips, her skin, her silken inky hair brushing below my shoulders.

When the water turned cold, we stepped out, but went into the other room and collapsed into the cream-coloured silken sheets, with only the silken sheet below me and Teela's silken skin above me. We roamed our hands over every inch of each other, so breathlessly caught in our hailstorm of passion that we failed to notice the edge of the bed, and with a startled yelp, I tumbled over the side and landed with a hollow 'thud' on the floor, yanking half of the bedding along with me. I was momentary startled, but as soon as both of us realized that no one was hurt, we both busted out laughing. Teela reached over the side of the bed and offered me a hand. "Careful there, Cindy," she teased as she helped me up. We were silent for a moment, but then seeing the pitifully drooping pile of bedding on the floor, we busted out laughing all over again. She pinched me lightly. "I make you so clumsy, but I love it," she told me with a smile.

"That's for sure," I answered. "Whenever I fall, I just get back up."

Teela leaned over and checked the bedside clock. "Wow, it's late now. Want to go make some dinner now?"

I nodded. "Absolutely," I agreed. "After enduring a few days of that awful hospital food, I'm famished."

Chapter Twenty-Three

I woke up early the next morning and looked over at Teela, who was sleeping on the other side of the bed. Her black inky hair was spread out across her pillow and she was facing me, her lips slightly parted and one of her arms extended. Man, she was so beautiful, even when she was asleep. I checked the clock and it said eight-thirty, so I didn't feel the need to get up. Ah, heck, I thought, I'd stay in bed a little longer. I did get up and staggered into the bathroom to swig some mouthwash, use the toilet, and wash my face off, but then I went back into the bedroom and slid back into bed. I was just so thankful to be back at home with Teela, with all the bad guys gone and no more major traumatic events going on. I hoped that we would never, ever have to go through anything like that again.

It was around ten when I felt Teela stirring beside me and woke up again. I rose out of bed, took a shower, got dressed in a black long-sleeved shirt and grey yoga pants, and went into the kitchen, preparing to make us some breakfast. I decided to whip up an apple pie to celebrate making it through all of our tough times. Fortunately, there happened to be a sack of apples in the refrigerator, which definitely weren't going to be used for anything else. I rinsed off the apples and turned on the radio before I got out the plate and the apple peeler. I hummed along to whatever song was on the radio as I shucked the peels off of the apples. I sort of lost myself in my work as I peeled and chopped and mixed up the filling. Soon after all of that, Teela stepped into the kitchen and bade me good morning. I turned, and she looked gorgeous as ever in a deep blue silky scoop-neck shirt and black leggings.

"You look real pretty this mornin', Teela," I told her in a soft voice.

She smiled. "Thanks, Cynthia," she answered, squeezing my shoulders, her scent filling the air around me in an ephemeral wind. "So do you."

She helped me prepare the rest of the pie, specifically the crust. Teela's pie crust was straight from heaven, flaky and delicate, not to oily, not too dry. She said that her aunt, who was a professional chef, taught her how to make pie crust, and she had been baking since her childhood. I finished chopping the apples and stuck the mixture in the microwave. While I waited for the apple filling to finish cooking, I watched Teela as she began preparing the crust. She stirred in all of the ingredients and then gently kneaded the newly formed dough with her long, slender fingers. Watching her intently at work was fascinating; she was so beautiful and worked with such ease and grace. Her dark inky hair was pulled back into a ponytail and her long lashes lowered. I couldn't help but to marvel at her skill. "You're a very talented baker," I told her as she rolled the crust thin and laid it in the pie pan.

She looked up at me with her signature ghost of a smile on her lips, her lashes flickering over her almond-shaped gray eyes for the briefest moment. She shrugged. "Well, I hope I am," she laughed.

Her musical laugh was a melody, her vibrant face full of life, her hands slim and strong as she worked with the newly formed crust.

"Teela," I breathed. "You're so beautiful; I just can't stand it."

She set down the crust and turned around. "Thank you, Cynthia," she all but whispered, her eyes slightly misty. "And you are too."

The dancing heat behind her eyes had me blushing ever so slightly. I tucked an errant strand of brown hair behind my ear and lowered my eyes. Sometimes she was so beautiful that it almost hurt to look at her, like the sun. We both just stood in silence, intermittently setting things out and every once and a while, we would lock eyes and it would be like a brush fire had spread throughout the house. I fumbled around, nearly breaking the plates in my hands when I caught Teela studying me in the pensive, methodical way that she thought about things. That was how she approached everything, thoroughly and pensively, and sometimes passionately. Being under her scrutiny was a jarring, breathtaking experience, and I felt that not only could she see through my clothes but also straight through my soul. I looked up and my lips parted slightly, involuntarily when I met her eyes. She wasn't staring at me but I could tell that she had been shaping me up, mind, body, and soul, with that artistic mind of hers.

"Something on your mind, Teela?" I asked her.

She smiled. "Something's always on my mind, I never stop thinking. What's on your mind, Cynthia?"

I looked down. "Well," I began sheepishly. "I think you could have a fair idea."

Suddenly, Teela's lavender scent surrounded me and she rested her hands on my hips. "You're blushing," she murmured, which made me blush even harder.

Just then, BEEEEP! The microwave dinged, signaling that the filling was done. Lightly as a feather, Teela squeezed my hips one more time, before relaxing her hands and turning away. "Gotta get this," she told me, opening the door to the microwave. "Want to make us some coffee?"

She dumped the filling into the crust she had prepared, and I fired up the old rickety coffee maker, which, I swear, had a temperament of its own. It hissed at me as I filled it and melted the handle of a plastic spoon which was too close to the heating pad. I mentioned this to Teela about my theory of it having a personality and she laughed genuinely. "Indeed, it seems to," she answered with a dainty little giggle, as she began chopping the thin dough slices to place in a lattice over the top of her creation. While she finished up and stuck the pie in the oven, I got out two coffee mugs and my favorite hazelnut creamer. Teela and I sat down at the table to wait for the pie and sipped our coffee. I had been thinking, what were Teela and I going to do? Yeah, I loved her, but did she want to stay here forever? I knew that I would drop it all just to be with her but maybe she didn't want that. The mere thought of losing her cut through to my core like a gleaming, newly sharpened saber.

She must have noticed my pained expression because she pointed it out. "Are you all right, Cynthia?" she asked softly.

I nodded. "I am," I answered. "I'm just thinking." She nodded, and we went back to listening to the radio, which was playing a soft song from a few decades ago. Finally, I broke the silence with my concern. "Teela?" I asked hesitantly. "What do you want to do, you know, in our future?"

Teela faced me. "Honestly, Cindy, I'm not totally sure what the future holds, but…"

My face fell. Here is where she was going to say goodbye. "But what?" I croaked.

"But I want to spend it with you," she answered.

"Oh, Teela!" I exclaimed softly. "That is what I want, too. You're all I want. Let's celebrate with some apple pie,"

We got the pie out of the oven and it was beautiful, with intricate latticework on top and creamy, spicy apple filling. The warm, inviting scent filled the kitchen and surrounded both of us with a fragrant cloud. When I took my first taste of the pie that Teela and I had made together, and it was like opening a door to heaven itself. The apples were sweet, with a hint of spicy cinnamon, and the crust was beautifully crafted, light and flaky but not too oily. Perfection.

"We should have a reception," I suggested to Teela. "And a commitment ceremony."

She nodded. "Of course," she answered. "I was thinking the same thing."

Shyly, I reached into my pocket and pulled out a ring that I'd picked out for my wedding when I was a young girl. Then I took her hand and slipped it onto her finger.

Surprisingly, she also reached into her pocket and pulled out a ring as well, sliding it onto my finger. We beamed at each other and clasped our hands together.

Chapter Twenty-Four

Teela and I decided not to wait for our ceremony and planned it for a few months in advance. We decided to have dinner at a ritzy restaurant and spend the night in a classy hotel. This was going to be our wedding, so to speak, so we decided not to waste any time planning. We both wanted to wear dresses, and so we bought identical ones, hers in black and mine in white, with some accents of grey. It was the perfect combination, me classic and plain, her dark and alluring, with a splash of grey to represent the black and white coming together. The little boutique was called A Night on the Town, and my neighbor Rose recommended it. She was newly married and said that the prices and quality were phenomenal. Before that, our luck was not so good. We tried a place that we had heard an ad for in the newspaper and everyone raved about it, but it turned out awfully. Here is how our first dress-shopping encounter went down: It was a clear, crisp winter Saturday afternoon, only slight flurries were falling. The place was on the other side of town but it was the only place we knew, called Silk n' Satin. As soon as we pulled up to the building, I turned to Teela. "Yup, this is gonna be expensive," I told her. "My wallet is in pain already."

Teela nodded. "Mine too," she answered. "But maybe they have some good clearance stuff."

I shut off the motor and pulled the keys out of the ignition. "Well, it's worth a shot," I commented. I hopped out of the driver's seat and walked around to Teela's side to open the door for her. That was something we always did for each other, whoever drove usually opened the door, but we switched off things like that. "My lady," I gallantly opened the door and helped her down like a knight in shining armor. Teela laughed merrily and squeezed my hand as we walked into the store.

Inside, the place was immaculate. Rows and rows of dresses of all shapes, sizes, and materials hung on racks and shoes lined the shelves. There was a rack in the corner labeled "Clearance."

There were a few other people in the store, a lot of women trying on wedding dresses, their fiancés right there with them, looking bored out of their minds. "Come on," I told Teela, motioning for her to follow me. "Let's check the clearance rack."

She followed me and we started sifting through the racks. At first, we didn't find anything. "What are you thinking?" I asked Teela.

She thought for a moment, before answering. "Well, let's just see what we can find," she answered. "I'm not sure yet." So we went back to searching, and gathered up a pile of a few possibilities, including a beautiful jade-green silk gown for Teela and a similar but not identical greyish one for me. I found a beautiful white shirtdress type of garment, the perfect balance between casual and dressy. It had beige accents around the neckline and hem. I wasn't much of a dress person but it looked pretty nice, best of the lot. Teela, on the other hand, when she stepped into that dusty-jade slip of sheer silk heaven, I nearly fainted.

"My god, you're stunning," I breathed.

She grinned at me. "You as well," she answered, just about knocking me dead. She squeezed my hand and I beamed at her and took her face in my hands, kissing her lightly.

Once we had what we wanted, we headed to the checkout. The dresses were expensive, but knowing how lovely Teela looked in that jade dress, I was willing to pay just about anything. I planned to secretly buy her a necklace made of pure jade and surprise her with it on our big day. When we got to the counter, there was a pinched-faced somewhat chubby blonde standing there. She flipped her long hair and gave us the once over. "Hi, did you find everything okay?" she asked, but sounded like she didn't give a shit.

"Yes we did," Teela answered a slight curtly, mirroring her tone without being rude.

"So, who's the lucky bride?" the girl asked as she checked the sizes and wrote stuff down in her ledger.

"Well, we both are," I answered.
She arched a perfect eyebrow. "Oh?" she asked. "Well, whose wedding is first?"

"Actually, we're engaged," I told her, and Teela and I smiled at each other.

The girl's expression was a mix of startled and disgusted. "Oh," she said sharply, not commenting any further. "We don't usually deal with homosexual patrons, but, okay." Then, she named the price.

"Wait a minute," I pointed out, ignoring her jab but ticked off at the fact that she just raised the price right in front of our eyes. "These were on the clearance rack, clearly marked 25% off."

The girl shook her head. "No, that sale ended yesterday," she replied snottily. "And besides, these don't apply."

Teela knew it was time for her to step in. "I'm afraid this exceeds our budget," she answered coolly, handing the dresses back to the salesgirl. Then, we turned around and walked out of the store. The girl called after us and tried to change our minds, but we strode out the door and let it close with a satisfying slam.

"Of all the nerve," I fumed on the way home, pounding my fist on the steering wheel.

Teela laid a gentle hand on my shoulder. "It's all right, Cynthia," she murmured. "That girl was a moron. Don't let it upset you."

"Enough dress shopping for one day," I sighed. "It's getting dark. Let's go chill at home. Movie night maybe?"

Teela smiled. "Sounds wonderful," she agreed.

Chapter Twenty-Five

This was it. The big day for Teela and me. We had booked a reservation at one of the fanciest restaurants in town, and were going to stay overnight in a ritzy hotel. It felt odd to know that in a few hours, I would be promising my life to someone else. Although we weren't having a formal church wedding, we would still be exchanging our vows to be together forever. As a kid, I had never thought much about what my wedding would be like, but I certainly never imagined that I would be walking down the aisle with Teela Grant.

Around nine, the telephone rang. I was in the bathroom, so Teela answered it. I could hear her talking but couldn't make out what she was saying. When I had finished up in the bathroom, I headed out, and Teela hung up, setting the phone back onto its cradle. She looked excited and slightly puzzled. "What is it?" I asked her. "Who was on the phone?"

"Oh, that was my aunt Ada," Teela answered. "She has a big house on the other side of town, and she wants us to come over in our dresses so she can see us on the big day."

I drew back, surprised. "Oh, really?" I asked. "Okay, I guess. When does she expect us?"

Teela shrugged. "I think she plans on one o'clock. She's really happy for us."

"What is she like?" I asked. "When you say Aunt Ada, sounds like she's ninety-four."

Teela smiled mysteriously. "You'll see," she answered. "I'm sure you'll like her."
I knew that if Teela liked her, I would too.

I went into my bedroom and got our dresses out of the garment bags. They were beautiful and identical in style, but mine was white and Teela's was black. Each dress had some silver accents around the waistline and neckline, with lace as well and it tied in the back. Teela and I helped each other get our dresses on, with all of the appropriate undergarments of course, including pantyhose, and then we donned our matching silver ballet flats. Teela helped me curl my hair and let it hang loose. I wasn't going to wear any makeup, it wasn't my style. Teela then retreated into the bathroom to get herself ready. When she emerged, I damn near dropped dead. She wore large silver hoops and red lipstick, her dress dipping down in the front to show a beautiful slice of pale, gleaming skin. Her hair was curled and pinned prettily out of her face and her lids were smoky with smudged kohl liner that made her look like a soap opera seductress or a glorious empress straight from the night. She was the Queen of the Night herself, and I was struck with silence and awe.

"Oh, my, Teela..." I whispered.

She beamed. And then she blushed a little. "You think I look that good?" she asked me.

I was lost for words. "Better than good," I murmured to her. "I think I might die if I can't kiss you right now, but I don't want to smear your makeup."

"Well, don't die, Cynthia," she replied, and before I knew it, I was airborne and ended up in her arms. She tilted my head back and crushed her mouth to mine, surrounding me and filling me with her scent, herself.

"Teela," I whispered, trailing my hands down her back and letting my fingers play in the slit at the back of her dress. We held each other for a moment, our eyes closed, before we finally pulled away and looked in the mirror. Sure enough, Teela's lipstick was smeared all over the place, and our hair was a bit windblown, but other than that we were ready. Teela wiped off her face and reapplied her lipstick, and I wiped my face as well. Soon, we were good as new again. It was about twelve-fifteen when we finally departed for Teela's aunt's house. Teela said that she would drive, because she knew the way.

The ride took about thirty-five minutes, as it turned out; Teela's aunt lived in a big house on the other side of town. We pulled up in front of a sprawling beige place with pretty blue shutters. I was surprised to see a beat-up blue pickup in the driveway. "Is that Ada's car?" I asked her, pointing to the truck.

Teela shrugged. "Probably," she answered. "Aunt Ada is pretty unique."
I pictured a loud, hard-of hearing stooped old woman who drove a pickup and smoked like a chimney, swore like a trucker.

Teela and I parked in the drive and got out, heading up the steps. I pressed the buzzer, and we waited for a moment, hearing some shuffling around inside before the lock disengaged.

The door was answered by a woman in her late thirties who must have been six foot one or taller. She had brown eyes, blond hair that she wore short like a boy's, with pink streaks, and her nose was pierced with a few hoops like an African tribal leader. She wore a dainty flowered top with a pair of skintight leather pants with a chain on them.

"Well , if it isn't my favorite niece," she boomed, clasping Teela in a hug and kissing her on both cheeks, her voice ringing through the room. After she had released Teela, she turned to me and stuck out a large hand and smiled at me brilliantly, her teeth bright as diamonds. "You must be Cindy," she announced. "I'm Auntie Ada."

I laughed and shook her hand. "I like you already, Auntie Ada," I told her. "Teela promised me that I would."

"I'm so happy you two could come see me," she beamed. "You're lovely together."

Then, she pulled us both into a hug. "Let me get a picture."

She pulled out a large camera and motioned Teela and me to stand against the wall. "Auntie Ada is a photographer," Teela explained to me.
Ada shrugged. "Well, I run my own business," she interjected modestly. After she snapped our pictures from every angle, she asked us if we wanted to come into the main part of the house to visit for a while. Teela and I glanced at each other and shrugged.

"Sure," we answered.

Ada opened the double doors that led from her entrance hall into the main foyer. The entire foyer was dark, and Teela and I were equally puzzled as to why all of the lights were off. I had barely taken time to absorb the vastness of the place when suddenly a chorus of people yelled "Surprise!" and strands of white lights popped on all over the room. Throngs of people stood up from behind furniture, flowers in hand. They each set their flowers down somewhere in the room, until the entire foyer was covered with light and flowers. Someone cued the music and Ada led us down the middle of the foyer. The crowd cheered as we walked by and threw handfuls of sweet scented jasmine rice and flower petals on us as we passed.

Ada led us into the next room, a massive dining hall with tables and tables of buffet food. I looked around in awe, unbelieving. I turned to Teela, wonder on my face. She smiled at my expression. "With Auntie it's always better to expect the unexpected," she commented, giving Ada a slap on the shoulder.

"Well," I answered. "There's unexpected, and then there's just… wow."

Teela nodded. "Yeah, this is unexpected even for her," she answered, and then she turned to Ada. "It's a gorgeous party, Auntie," she told her, and Ada pulled her into a hug.

"Thanks, sugar," she answered sincerely, beaming at her niece and me as well. "I'm so proud of you two for deciding to commit to each other like this; it is a real act of courage. Come, now, I want you to meet someone."

Ada led us through the room that was filled with people; she seemed to be looking for someone. Finally, she waved across the room, and someone came toward us. At first, the woman was too far away to see in the dim light, but as she neared, I saw that she was also as tall as Ada, taller actually with about four-inch stilettos and a dress that looked like it was made out of neon electrical tape. She was a black woman with exotic eyes and a tribal hair wrap with what looked like dreadlocks spilling down her back. The dress struggled to maintain her massive chest, but other than that, she was slim. The woman clacked closer in her heels and put her arm around Ada.

"Hi, honey," she said, her voice was low and melodic with what sounded like a thick Irish brogue, which was ultimately strange considering her ethnicity.

Ada turned to us, and presented the woman proudly. "Cynthia, this is my girlfriend, Carstairs."

I was surprised but also not surprised that Teela's aunt was one of us. Ada grinned as she finished the introduction. "This is Cynthia, and of course you remember my niece, Teela," she told Carstairs.

"Of course, it's great to see you, Teela," Carstairs answered with a smile, hugging Teela and then hugging me too. "Pleasure to meet you, Cynthia."

I liked her immediately. "You too," I answered. "And hope you don't mind me asking, is Carstairs your real name?"

She smiled. "Yes, it is," she answered. "Carstairs McKinley. I am originally from Macaroon, but I was adopted by an Irish family when I was a baby. I embrace my heritage!"

"I can see that," I told her. "You're a pretty interesting woman. I see how you and Ada get along."

She and Ada smiled at each other, clearly with love in their eyes. "Yup," she answered. "That's for sure."

Eventually, they excused themselves to go check on the appetizers, leaving Teela and I on our own. We stood around for a while, then got some food and sat down. I wished that there could be an aisle for us just like there was for any other couple. When I told this to Teela, she agreed wistfully. Eventually, Ada came back and told Teela to come with her for a moment. Carstairs simultaneously appeared and led me away as well. When I asked what was going on, she simply smiled mysteriously and told me that I would soon find out. She took me into the bathroom and touched up my makeup, until I looked perfect. It only took a few moments, and when she was finished she led me to the front of the foyer and told me to just stand there. Then, she walked away.

"Wait…" I called after her, but she kept walking. What the heck? I thought. Suddenly, all of the music shut off and the lights dimmed to absolute blackness. I stood there, bewildered, and the crowd murmured, confused as well. Suddenly, thousands of tiny lights illuminated all around the dome-shaped ceiling, and the room was bathed in a pretty golden glow. As the lights went on, the crowd went silent. Suddenly, one of Teela and my favorite songs started playing, the bass thrumming through the house but not too loud. It started softly at first but grew louder, and I could see the crowd parting from the other end of the room. As I stood there, I could see Teela gliding toward me, a lantern in her hand and a genuine beaming smile on her face, radiant. I couldn't help but to break into tears as she swept closer, the lantern light illuminating her beautiful face. She was really walking down the aisle.

Someone gave me a gentle shove from behind, and I couldn't help but to walk towards her with all of my heart. When we met in the middle of the crowd, I took her face in my hands and kissed her, and the crowd cheered and threw jasmine rice and pale pink rose petals on us, and glitter rained from the ceiling, soaking us as the lights changed to a pink glow and a dance song started. Teela and I wrapped our arms around each other and began to sway to the music, and soon other people started to dance as well. We danced and danced, she closed her kohl-lined smoky eyes and pressed her cheek to mine, her scent winding its way around me. We became one person, closing our eyes and swaying together, her curves pressing deliciously to mine and making me ache to be closer to her. "Did you know about the dancing?" I asked her. She smiled, her pretty lids still closed.

"I had a fair idea," she murmured. "But Auntie came up with it. She and Carstairs had a party like this when they made their commitment. I mentioned to her how much we wanted to walk down the aisle, but she surprised us,"

"Your aunt is so nice," I told her. "Did she come up with this herself? How did she pay for it all?"

"Carstairs is a lawyer, and Ada is a self-employed wedding photographer, both very successful. Ada didn't go to college. In fact, she dropped out of high school and moved out when she was sixteen. Apparently, as soon as they heard of our engagement they started planning. Auntie was the first one I told."

***

We had a wonderful time dancing and chatting with Aunt Ada and Carstairs and the other assorted guests. After a few hours, we left, because we were going out to dinner and going on our respective honeymoon that night at the ritziest hotel in town. The brunch at Auntie Ada's was very light, so we would still have room for dinner.

Chapter Twenty-Six

After Teela and I left the little reception at Auntie Ada's house, we went home to get some rest before we headed off to dinner and our honeymoon night. The lunch at Ada's was good, but luckily we didn't eat too much of it, so we still had room for our ritzy dinner for that night. "Wow, that was quite a fancy shindig," I remarked to Teela as we were in the car en route back to our house.

Teela nodded. "Completely," she agreed. "It was lovely, though. I still can't believe Auntie and Carstairs paid for the whole thing themselves."

I was still astounded at how large Teela's aunt's house was. "Me either," I agreed, and while we were stopped at a red light, I reached over and squeezed Teela's hand. "I'm so glad that we got to walk down the aisle, though, it means a lot to me," I told her.

Teela turned to me, her misty gray eyes deep with emotion. "It means a lot to me as well, Cynthia," she returned softly. "It felt right in a way that it never has before."

I nodded solemnly. "When I saw you gliding towards me in all of that black lace, well, I just knew that you're the only one I want."

Teela's face shone in a way that was incomprehensible by English speech alone. She simply blinked. "Thank you," she whispered.

We sat in warm, deep, heartfelt silence pondering our decision to become permanently committed, until the light changed from red to green. Teela ever so gently extricated her hand so that she could rest it on the wheel. "Sorry, I gotta drive," she grinned, and we shared a smile. I was so overcome with happiness at finding my true self and the one I truly loved, I felt free like I never had before. On sheer impulse, I took a handful of silver glitter and flung it out the window, watching the tiny silver particles swirl and dance through the breeze that streamed behind the car.

When we finally got home, we alighted and headed into the house, deciding to take a rest before the evening festivities in a few hours. The impromptu soiree at Auntie Ada's had us just a slight tired out. Luckily the house was pretty much in order, and we had packed our bags for our weekend away at the hotel that accompanied the ritzy restaurant where we planned to dine that evening. We were glad to be rid of our dresses for a few hours, even though we were going to get all dressed up once more in a few hours. Our venue was the Clifton Manor, about a half-hour drive from our home, located on a pretty little lake. We had picked it because I wanted a fancy dinner and Teela wasn't fond of traveling. It was the best place in town, expensive, yes, but it was worth it, because after all this was our wedding night.

Soon, after our brief rest and last minute preparations, it was time to don our dresses again to go out to dinner. And this was just as exciting as it was the first time, and I was already craving the signature Clifton Manor vanilla bean cheesecake, could already taste it on my tongue. I expressed this sentiment to Teela, and she agreed wholeheartedly. The third reason that we chose Clifton Manor for our honeymoon was just that: the divinely delicious vanilla bean cheesecake.

When we were ready, it was nearly four-thirty. We got into the car and I turned on the radio. One of our favorite eighties bands was playing, mellow swing lounge music filtered through the speakers and calmed our nerves. The drive over to Clifton Manor was scenic, winding through country that we hadn't often frequented. In about exactly a half-hour, just as planned, we arrived at the manor. The hotel was secluded in a grove of evergreen and overlooking a calm mauve-blue lake. The building was made of stone and contained four stories, complete with the foyer where the restaurant was housed, some tables out on a balcony over the water. There was ample space for parking, and despite the fanciness of the place, parking was free.

I parked the car and opened the door, thankful for the nice new asphalt beneath my feet. I clacked over to the other side and opened Teela's door for her, offering my hand to help her down. She beamed as she took my proffered arm and we walked up to the main door together, arm-in-arm. Her inky ebony hair was pinned lightly out of her face, half-up, with curls spilling over her bare shoulders and down her back, and the sweeping hem of her black lace dress trailed behind, giving her the air of the Queen of the Night. I reached the door first and held it open for her as we stepped into the dimly lit cozy lobby. There were leather easy chairs arranged around a faux fireplace and mock gas lamps lined the walls, giving it a homey, cabin type of feel. We had just stepped in the door when we were approached by a man in a suit. He offered us a wide smile. "Hi, I'm John Pierce, owner of the Clifton Manor," he extended his hand and gave us each a hearty handshake. "Welcome!"

We smiled as we shook hands with him. He led us over to the desk and asked our names. He looked up in his catalog and handed us the keys to our room, number 314. "Lake view," he assured us. "King size bed."

"Perfect," I answered.

He snapped his fingers and bellowed, "Steven!" Just then, a skinny bellhop appeared, ready to get our luggage. I pointed out which car was ours and he headed out with the luggage cart to fetch it from the trunk. While we were waiting, the owner remarked that we looked very nice and asked us what our occasion was.

"We're engaged for life," I told him. "This is our honeymoon night."

He beamed. "Congratulations!" he exclaimed. "I'm so glad that you two chose this hotel to celebrate. Good luck, ladies!"

We thanked him, and he excused himself to tend to some business behind the desk, saying once more that he was pleased to meet us and hoped we had a pleasant stay.

"What a lovely place," Teela remarked, looking around. "I love the whole evergreen-cabin theme."

I smiled. "Me too," I agreed. "I knew that it was the right place to come."

Just then, Steven the bellhop returned with our bags and told us that he locked up the car for us. We followed him into the elevator with the cart, and he pressed the button for the third floor. When our destination was reached, we got off and headed to our room, shortly down the dimly lit hallway. Gas lanterns lined the hallways as well, and the furnishing was comfortable. I pulled the key card out of my pocket and stuck it in the slot. Steven waited for us to get our bags off the cart and then he turned to go. I pulled a dollar bill out of my pocket and tipped him, for which he was extremely grateful. Once Teela and I got into the room, we closed locked the door and surveyed our new abode. The room was simple but beautifully done, with a deep forest-green bedspread on the king-size bed, a shiny pine headboard, white curtains, and a deep green carpet. The bathroom was off to the side with a spacious walk-in shower and there was a large flat screen on the wall in front of the bed. We got fixed up for dinner soon, since our reservation was at six.

Once Teela and I were ready for dinner, we headed downstairs, arm-in-arm once again. When we got down to the restaurant, it was beginning to darken, the glow of the gas lanterns creating a romantic atmosphere. The entire theme of the restaurant was a homey cabin, lodge type thing that went along with the rest of the hotel. We waited by the sign that stated, "Please wait to be seated."

After a few moments, a woman in a Clifton Manor shirt approached and asked us if we had a reservation.

"Washek and Grant, six o'clock," I told her, and she smiled widely.

"Right this way, ladies," she directed us to a cozy little two-top table right next to the window where we could clearly see the sun beginning to set over the lake. "Your server will be with you shortly."

She handed us each a menu and bustled off. The dining room was pretty much secluded, with one or two other couples down at the other end of the room. Teela and I opened up our menus and looked over all of the decadently delicious choices. "I've heard that their Tabbouleh is really good," Teela remarked to me.

"What's that?" I asked her curiously. Teela was big on ethnic foods, so she often came up with some strange dishes, but they always seemed to be good.

"It's an Arabian salad," she explained to me. "Made with bulgur, tomato, parsley, garlic, onion, cucumber, et cetera. Look on page 4 of the menu, under salads."

I flipped open my menu and studied the description. "Yeah, looks great," I agreed. "Something different, I'll have some too."

Soon, a pleasant-faced brown-haired woman arrived at our table with a notepad in her hand. "Hi, I'm Sharon, and I'll be serving you tonight," she smiled warmly at us and flipped open her order pad. "May I get you ladies anything to drink?"

"Two glasses of Chianti, please," I requested, and Teela nodded with a faint smile.

"I'll be back soon with your drinks," Sharon told us. "Have you decided on an appetizer yet or still thinking about it?"

We told her that we had decided on two helpings of Tabbouleh to start, and she jotted it down on her paper. After we had finished ordering our salad and drinks, Sharon departed with a smile. When she had gone, I continued to peruse the menu to decide on the main meal. I was just about to suggest the grilled vegetable pizza plate when I glanced up, and found Teela studying me as she did at times. It was flattering but unnerving, and I never knew what she was thinking. "Something on your mind?" I asked her quietly, breaking the silence.

She shook her head. "No, not really," she answered softly. "I was just thinking of how you have this little curve to your lips. Pardon me, I often draw in my mind, it's an exercise."

I smiled, blushed a little. "Well, I hope it's not a caricature," I joked, and Teela grinned as well. Talking about drawing mental pictures was dangerous, though, because those pictures that I may have come up with of Teela could cause a wildfire and make me unable to think straight for the rest of the night. She knew it, too, and we both knew what awaited us after our dinner was finished. I ached to touch her but I knew that I would go up in flame the second that I did, and all control would be lost.

Just then, Sharon returned with our drinks and salads. "Here you go, ladies, enjoy," she chirped, before she bustled off to take care of another table.

When she had departed, I lifted my glass. "I propose a toast," I announced quietly. "To us, Teela, you and me forever."

Teela's misty eyes were quiet and pensive as she lifted her glass, clinking it gently against mine. "To us, Cynthia," she echoed. "Forever."

We paused and took our first sips of our drinks, savoring the fresh, sharp taste.
After our toast moment was finished, we said a quick grace over our banquet and dug in. Surprisingly enough the Tabbouleh was pretty good. I expressed this sentiment to Teela, who returned with a good-natured "told ya so."

The crisp bulgur had a very unique taste but was complemented perfectly by the assortment of vegetables. Soon, Sharon returned and asked if we were ready for a main course. After some debating, Teela and I decided to split a dish of olive-oil grilled summer tofu and vegetables with an overlay of seasoned, fried cappellini noodles. Sharon told us that it was the vegetarian special this week, with a special discount price. When our main course came, it was steaming hot and smelled delicious, but at the last minute, I told her to box it up for us and just bring the vanilla bean cheesecake. "I've been simply dying for a slice of that cake!" I exclaimed, and Sharon laughed. She said that many patrons feel the same way, and that she would certainly box up the main course for us.

"Well, we'll have dinner in style tomorrow night," I remarked to Teela, and she smiled.

"I just want that cake," she said wistfully, and we both chuckled.

"Yeah, I think we agree on the cake," I added, and soon our wish came true, and Sharon brought out a special platter and two plates.

"Here it is, ladies, le piece de le resistance."

Teela and I each took a slice of the decadent vanilla bean cake, complete with a scoop of fresh berries on the side. "What kind of berry sauce did you get?" I asked Teela.

"Raspberry," she answered. "What about you?"

"Blueberry," I replied. "Wanna try some? It's good,"

"Sure," she replied, and I took a forkful of cake and lifted it to her lips. She took it delicately and closed her eyes as she tasted it. "Mm, that's good," she remarked softly. "Want a bite of mine?"

"Yes," I answered, and she followed my lead and lifted her fork to my lips. "Wow, the raspberry is good, too," I commented.

"Yeah?" she asked softly, trailing her fingernail along her lip in the way that set my reserve on fire. The most beguiling thing about her was her seductive artlessness. She never tried hard to fry my mind, she simply did without effort.

We slowly ate our cake, savoring every bite as it grew dark outside. The diner had gotten somewhat busier since the beginning, but mainly over at the bar counter. The restaurant itself was pretty deserted except for the two of us, but over at the bar, a bunch of rowdy men were hooting and hollering. When we had finally polished off the last of our slim slices of sheer heaven and secured the bill, we bade Sharon good-night and rose to head back up to our room.

"That was a delicious dinner," I remarked as Teela and I boarded the elevator up to our room.

She nodded. "Indeed," she agreed. We walked hand-in-hand to our room, then I momentarily broke away to open the door.

Once we were in the room, I turned on one of the dim bedside lanterns and went to go close the shades. "What a lovely view," I commented as I closed the blinds. "Such a serene lake. How about a little music?" I cranked the dial on the bedside radio to a pleasant eighties-lounge station, adjusting the volume so that it provided a background but wasn't blaring. I was standing at the desk, facing the clock and the radio, and my hand reached out to dim the lights.

"Come here, Cynthia," I heard Teela whisper gently, her voice winding through the near darkness. I turned around and could barely make out the shape of her, but I smelled lavender and passion in the air.

"I will," I murmured back, and before I knew it, I was in her arms. I tilted her face up and admired the way that the moonlight slanted over her smoky eyelids and dusky hair. "You're so beautiful, my Teela," I whispered, and I closed my eyes and gently crushed my lips to hers. She tasted like lavender, cake, and passion, intoxicating. My head was swimming with nothing but her. I buried my face in the crook of her neck and her errant hands swished over my sides and back, until she found the straps holding up my dress. "Should I help you?" I whispered, and she shook her head. I felt her fingers working at the ties and before I knew it, whoosh, my dress was on the floor. I slid my hands along the back of her dress, cupping her curves through the lace, and with shaking fingers I reached for the ties that held the fabric in place. I struggled with the ties for a while, my fingers made of lead. "Sorry," I whispered. "I'm not having much luck here."

Teela smiled. "It's all right, Cynthia," she murmured. "No need to rush, we have all night." Finally, I managed to free the bow and her dress swished to the floor with a quiet breath of silk. Now, there were only two mere scraps of fabric between us, her black lace thong and my white silken bikini bottom. We let our hands rove over each other's smooth bare skin and we danced in each other's arms, lips locked, hair everywhere, until we spun onto the bed and I pulled her down on top of me. Her inky hair was falling softly all around my face and she trailed her smooth glass-like hands up my legs. It wasn't long before the last scraps of cloth had gone to the wind, and there was a pile of discarded clothing on the floor, and nothing but Teela's burning hot skin against mine, my hands in her hair, lips everywhere as our passion threatened to overcome us. I reverenced every inch of her in every way that I could, her smoky, husky murmurs urging me on. Finally, late into the night, the aching tidal wave collapsed into itself and I completely gave my everything to Teela, murmuring her name as a mantra as she sent me sailing out of my mind and right down into the molten core of the universe and up to the farthest galaxy all at once. There was nothing as completely searing and satisfying as her hot, skilled hands and her utterly intoxicating taste. Finally, when all of our energy had finally been depleted and the supernova burned to the core and flamed out, we collapsed in each other's arms, heavily drenched in sweat and flushed with ecstasy. Before we fell asleep, I thought of everything that Teela and I had been through together and how we truly had come to love each other. Maybe some people wouldn't have been able to acknowledge a bond like this, but I felt truly free for once in my life. I leaned over and brushed Teela's hair out of her face. "Good night, beautiful," I whispered. "I love you with all of my heart."

"You saved me from my past and my misery, Cynthia, and I love you too," she murmured sleepily.

We kissed gently one more time and wished each other good night, drifting to sleep. Right then, right there, I fell home in her arms, knowing I never had to let go.

The End

Sara J. Kuhrman

If you enjoyed <u>Lost and Found</u> by Sara J. Kuhrman, there are more books… Look for:

THE HALLOWED HALLS

By Sara J. Kuhrman

Meagan Lucien has always had to fight for what she wants, often having to be reckless to the point of callousness. The only way that she can hide the pain of her past is by fulfilling her every desire. So, when she develops an insatiable attraction to her sexy, charismatic calculus professor, Terrence Reid, she endeavors to seduce him, unexpectedly falling in love with him along the way.

But when a tragedy strikes in Terrence's family, things change drastically for both of them. Terrence withdraws and blames himself for what happened, and Meagan becomes a social outcast, being forced to mature and face the truth about her character. Will their lives be consumed in the web of deceit and tragedy or can they find the light at the end of the tunnel?

Coming soon in Fall/Winter 2015

About The Author

Sara J. Kuhrman is a witty, eccentric young lady who is known for always making her own way in life. She loves writing, especially melodramatic stories of people bonding in spite of tragedy or criticism, with a particular penchant for alluring, dark-haired heroines in her lesbian romance novels. In her free time, Sara enjoys reading, taking walks and analyzing the ways of the world, always dreaming up another story line.

www.ingramcontent.com/pod-product-compliance
Lightning Source LLC
Chambersburg PA
CBHW070333130626
46556CB00007B/2835